Shame Baseball

Shame Baseball

Jeff Newburg

RESOURCE *Publications* · Eugene, Oregon

SHAME BASEBALL

Resource Publications
An Imprint of Wipf and Stock Publishers
199 W. 8th Ave., Suite 3
Eugene, OR 97401

www.wipfandstock.com

PAPERBACK ISBN: 978-1-7252-6743-5
HARDCOVER ISBN: 978-1-7252-6744-2
EBOOK ISBN: 978-1-7252-6745-9

Manufactured in the U.S.A.   07/17/20

Not *For Winnie and Augie.*
To you, may this shame story sound like it's from the fuckin moon.

For Kelly.
By the time these words are printed, may love tower over our present hurts.

Contents

I

1

Fathers

FATHER, YOU'VE TOLD ME you don't understand me, that you can't see my words and deeds as those of a Christian Man. Of specific concern, you've told me, are my Obama votes and dim view of capitalism. The confounding is precisely mutual—I cannot understand your actions as inspired by Christ; I have only acted as I have because of my faith. I haven't recently brought up my doubts about your theopolitical positions, not because I ceased to have them but because I've thought the conversation wouldn't do any good. And also I didn't want to hurt you. And also I haven't, since my mother's death, had the emotional bandwidth to sit under your judgment—to be processed by it, tireless machine. And so in our time together this last year or so, I've just sat there as you hold forth on any matter, presuming my silence is agreement.

This is uncomfortable enough at the beginning of a conversation. But as you move through point A and, seeing no disagreement on me, drive on and on to Z, by which point you're thinking I too believe the Civil War was fought over states' rights or churches that neglect to teach the *headship* of husbands over wives are *evil*—this has been a deathly anxious experience. Which I can no longer tolerate. I believe my reticence has allowed you to hurt me more deeply, that the collective reticence of my cohort has allowed you and those in yours to speak, and do, and vote, great damage upon us all.

I believe in this time with poison all around us the right thing to do, at long last, is to better elucidate our disagreement, or if such precision and charity of thought is beyond me, to at least stop pretending it doesn't exist.

There is so much grievance in me. I don't want there to be. I also want to live my best life now. I hope my anger doesn't come across as, and isn't, hate. I do love you and want the best for you. But it may be hard for me to avoid saying hateful things to the man who taught me, I've only recently come to know, to hate myself. I'm sure that comes as a shocking accusation, and intentionally hurtful. It was a shock to me to realize I've hated myself. My protests to the contrary have been such a massive part of my internal dialogue, just so I could get by, I see now. I can't imagine you accepting you taught me this hate. I can't imagine your slowing down to examine the roots of the constant self-criticism, that regular swearing at yourself under your breath I've seen you do. But I'll try to let go of my need to convince you, as I've tried to let go of my need to be cared for by you, or even cared about, to stop being surprised by your regression into shaming me on all matters, down to the level of what I eat for breakfast, up to the level of who I am as a *Christian Man*.

As I've let go of a relationship with you, in any meaningful sense of the word, I haven't been able to get rid of the voice of constant self-criticism. I've stopped denying it's your voice when I catch myself swearing under my breath, that the grimace on my face when I look myself in any mirror is your grimace. I can't continue to censor the feelings I have about you. These censorships have only served to incubate the self-hate, which has grown to monstrous proportions, smothering what occasional health my thought life contained.

My self-hate was quite painful even when I was doing everything *right*. Now that I've left my church and my marriage is ending, it's of a magnitude that swallows my coping. I have to find another way.

I don't want to think of God as I know you, giving the good things only conditionally, before they are withdrawn arbitrarily. But my recent experience with you and other father figures, in the church and elsewhere, has me thinking that way.

I've resolved to write this accounting of myself in this time that I'm most inclined to judge myself, to get it all down on paper, hoping that by the end I'll better understand which voice is me, which is you and which, if there's anything left, is God. Honesty about who I am and how I feel will be brand new between us. So much all at once, after speaking so little in recent years, and even then speaking of so little of actual substance, may come as quite a shock. If I were a more psychologically mature person, I'd probably divine a kinder and gentler way. But I am not mature, I realize. I am a little boy. I'm sorry for the shocking; I acknowledge my complicity in your impression that we're okay.

No thought here is finished; I am in process. Whatever my discernable beliefs are here, they will certainly be unsystematic. To present these unvarnished pieces of myself is to invite you to pick them—me—apart. And I accept that. I'm sorry if this is hard for you but it is necessary for me.

I know this accounting will not improve my standing in your eyes. I imagine the moments I imply your accountability for the state of things will leave you defensive and accusatory. Maybe I'm counting on it. Maybe I want, if hope of an actual relationship is dead, a clean break.

I am, if you'll recall, your elder in the faith, my youth group conversion anticipating your turn toward evangelicalism, which you've called your *salvation moment*, by two years.

And so I *deserve* to be heard out, Father. Unstop your ears.

2

I Feel the Need to Say,

as I exhume my anger toward you, Father, there was an artist in you. You told me once you decided to move to Arizona when you were a teenager visiting your sister in college at the U of A. You looked up at that night sky and those mountains and the cacti amid the night bugs buzzing and made a promise to your future self you'd one day breathe desert air nightly. You told me this just a few years ago, after three decades of showing me a man who'd mastered his emotions into oblivion.

It felt the same as when you told me your father had been a talented artist as a teenager, that he was going to go to art school, and only moved onto the insurance executive track—the only way I'd known him—after being mocked mercilessly by his Midwestern male cohort. You told me this years after his death, which occurred while I was discovering the art school within my college. You somehow didn't figure I'd want to know I wasn't alone in our family.

I also remember floating with you. At age twelve, our arms crossed with themselves across from each other, on both sides of a blue foam pool float. You looked at me with openness and care as you gave me a sex talk, containing no facts I hadn't know for years. I was so petrified I got a burn on my arm with a hole in the middle, where a drop of water lay still enough to sunscreen me. Your compassion was so unexpected, and on so grave a topic. I didn't know what to do. This was a couple years before your evangelical turn and a couple years after your divorce from my mother. Looking back at this period, I imagine you'd found compassion for yourself and your sexuality. This time between the judgment you used to keep yourself in line in your first marriage and the judgment you would find soon in the church. I see beauty in that floating moment now, for you.

You reached out to touch my arm as you asked if I had any questions. I, a boy starved of your touch, who wanted nothing more than your acceptance, would have in that moment vaporized your arm with lasers from my eyes, if force of will and fear and embarrassment could manifest lasers.

I have more anger toward you, more unforgiveness, than toward my abusive brother, my neglectful and alcoholic mother, my wife-beating alcoholic stepfather. I imagine this feels very unjust to you and I do feel guilty about it. Your religious hardlining kept you from such abuses.

But none of them pretended perfection. And so they have let me grieve their failures. Perhaps forgiveness, or my way of it at least, requires an accounting. I get the impression you couldn't tolerate that. You must skip past it, shouting "washed white as snow" with fingers in your ears, frustrated the aggrieved party can't just move on to your salvation moment as The Lord has. I wonder if you will literally skip pages of this accounting, snooping for the redemptive turn.

3

Preaching

I AM NO LONGER a pastor, Father. An *associate* pastor. Alright, self-deprecation, one of *three* associate pastors, at Church of the Redeemed, Los Angeles.

The head pastor, Steve, whose hand you've shaken, preaches forty Sundays a year, leaving each of us associates one Sunday per quarter. My slot in the fall quarter was coming up.

A month before, I'd stepped down from leading the artists' community we called the subchurch. Steve had called this decision "sudden." In that reserved church and with Steve, a former bonds trader, "sudden" was a weighty criticism indeed, intoned with the same fatherly reproach of "political," after I preached on "God, Father to the Refugee," in 2015, after that "rapists and murderers" bit from the man you voted for.

This time Steve was right. I really fell apart on him, myself, the subchurch.

Without my biggest job there, my *calling* of leading the subchurch, I was struggling with what my role at Redeemed could be. And the congregation of fifteen-hundred across three service times at our east- and west-side locations was there, waiting in the pews of my mind, for me to deliver The Word on Sunday.

By Monday both associates had offered to sub in for me; by Tuesday Pastor Steve had as well. I struggled all week with what I could honestly write and preach from where I was standing, slipping, spiritually. I finally stayed up all night Saturday to write this.

I often divert from my prepared text. But that Sunday it was all on paper as I meant it and so my writing is a faithful record. I won't indicate the uncomfortable coughs and whispers, the muffled mumbles coming from the congregation as I delivered it. For all I know that was all in my head; God knows I have thoroughly internalized—and reprojected—judgment from all around me by now. I'm less sure about much of my beliefs now than when I preached this and I blush at what is certainly the preachiest sermon I ever delivered. It is also digressive and more than a little indulgent, as my goodbyes often are. But it sent me on my path. And so now that I've thoroughly apologized to you for the failings in my craft and of my person, here is my last sermon.

∾

This won't be easy to say, but I do feel called to share it with you. Please put up with me.

I was in a coffee shop two days after the presidential election of 2016, all of us white folks crestfallen. I haven't told anyone this except my wife and my best friend, didn't think it would instill your confidence in me and, I confess, I care a great deal what you all think of me.

My anger and guilt had me rushing to get my application materials together for Harvard's Kennedy School of Government, thinking I had better become a politician. Or something. Forgive the impulsivity: I did not, as you can see, move to Cambridge. Forgive my foolishness: a minister who could never make it past number three on the depth chart deciding to go to Harvard and launch a political career. The righteous anger of that moment was intoxicating, if in fact less than righteous. I did not gain admittance and so I wasn't forced to deal with the temptation of that success. Mercy there.

I wasn't out of place writing application essays in that shop. As most of you know, Los Angeles coffee shops on weekdays are full of people writing screenplays in silence. But on that day, this shop became more like the coffee shop of my mind, although that picture is set in a logging town—I myself on my way to go log—all of us behaving more like townspeople there for the human engagement than as islands of the gig economy, talking the how could it *and* what can I *of the thing. One of the baristas, a black man who'd been involved with Black Lives Matter for some time, was FINE.*

"I'm not surprised," he said, pity and compassion in his shrug.

The white rage that had remained on the periphery of my consciousness had daily poked at his, unshielded by white privilege. An aside: if the phrase white privilege *makes you anxious, scared or angry, I hope you'll listen up rather than shut down. That anxiety, fear and anger are the parts of myself I'm preaching to.*

Standing across from the barista's clear-eyed stare, I felt dumb and numb: the needle had moved so much further than I knew, a feeling I'd already felt, in anxiously rising increments, after the primary campaign, the nomination, the general campaign. I had felt more and more like a fool and now, finally, exactly like one.

On that day, that barista didn't hesitate to dispense advice, telling people: come to a meeting; get involved. The reactions were guilty winces, masking outright repulsion. We are aghast and engaged if we can do it within our existing frames, from our phone or degreed in it by our institutions; if we have to show up to a meeting at the old rugged community center, which existed before we came and will after we're gone, where our place is to sit and listen, then the folks sitting in a coffee shop in the middle of the day are suddenly too busy.

Forgive me. I don't aim to offend; I am the offender I'm most concerned with.

I am trying to find the honesty in me now, or maybe refine it, smelt out the many little lies of my culture and of our church subculture, grown into me, proved now by this electoral end product, pernicious enough to stack up into the Big Lies.

This waking political cartoon—how else to articulate my level-11 evergreen shock at the sight of Trump beside a presidential seal?—is not my only context. I am a husband and a Christian pastor at this American church. I am attempting to live out my Christian faith amid this. I realize my way might not be what you would choose but I am trying. And I believe the way of my struggling is worth hearing.

Back to that day. This question wouldn't release me: if most of the white folks in that coffee shop deserved a scoff for their implicit role in this fresh mess, what is it the white American Christian pastor deserves, or—less shame, please—ought to do about it?

As I've struggle to grow during this time, I've felt myself growing out of the church, the American evangelical church I have known, at least. We can parse the E-word to death. In self-defense I want to. I want to tell myself that our particular church is a loving and dedicated one, which went more like 81% against Trump than 81% for him, as did white evangelicals broadly. I want to tell myself our head pastor is a faithful, literate, sensitive and complex human. I want to tell myself we are capable of moral ambiguity and are combatting shame, not feeding it.

But I cannot tell myself that LGBTQ children of God are embraced—loved as they may be—in our church. I can't tell myself that our denomination allows women to be ordained. We are many good things; a church whose egalitarianism has graduated into the middle of the twentieth century is not one of them. In a time where evil ethoses are incubating and multiplying with such alarming speed, the snail's pace of our church's cultural evolution is a less and less passive concern.

It may not be true, even before the embarrassment of 2016, that very many in our church embraced the label evangelical. But there is no doubt the evangelical movement fathered and shaped my faith and the faith of most of us here, its categories shaping our personal theological and psychological forms as surely as it did this church's theological stances, said and—artfully, lovingly—unsaid. We have been, in pride, guilt, shame and ambivalence, an evangelical church.

∽

There are better humans than I who will remain at our church. Perhaps they mount the defense I have: evangelical is used more now as a political signifier (anti-abortion, pro-gun) than it is a serious religious one. To gather data on self-identified evangelicals is not to gather data on practicing Christians. But I believe this deflects; deflecting is the opposite of the medicine I think we need.

It deflects because the signifier grew from the signified at some point, the fruit from a particular tree: we that took a homeless, crucified Palestinian servant-king and painted portraits of a handsome and stately white fellow, founded a theology of prosperity and might. I don't think white portraits of Jesus are a big lie; Christ is for all people and all people should image themselves in Him. But you keep on painting that portrait, you make that portrait the rule, and eventually Jesus is 6'4" and ripped, is holding Trump's bill-signing hand, is, if not the author of the second amendment, certainly the one who inspired its inerrancy. Forgive me my digressions. And my anger. I acknowledge it is not all righteous.

∽

I've served our church for thirteen years as a pastor, longer as a member and lay leader. I'm not certain there is a better church out there. I know that those who disagree with me are loving not despite their theology but because of it, imperfect as any theology will be. But. I now see that issues of inclusion within the church were on my periphery, pre-piercing. I modeled where I felt

I ought, stood up when I thought I could, but I did not treat these issues as essential; if I had I wouldn't have been able to stay in a place where they're not treated, in word and deed, as essential. Since they became essential to me, I've been in agony not doing anything about them. I have to stop the agony even if I'm trading it for the agony of loneliness. I know I will miss you, Family.

∿

I don't want to ghost, as many of my artist peers have already. If we young(er) members don't speak up about why it is we're leaving or why it is getting harder and harder to stay, American churches may presume they just need to get back to fiddling with the worship team's drumset to organ ratio.

Family, I can't shake this: I don't know how to read the Christ of the gospels as anything other than radically inclusive; our church is, on its face, more exclusive than most clubs I know of; our congregation made up nearly entirely of well put-together white and Asian folk with advanced degrees. In downtown Los Angeles, we have no geodemographic excuse for this state. The American evangelical church, on the whole, is less diverse still.

No amount of proof-texting singular sentences of exclusion, self-justifying of the status quo as they may be, makes the gospels' picture of Christ any less radically inclusive. He is always there, in quadruplicate, flinging wide the doors of the Kingdom. He tells stories about inviting homeless strangers—good and bad, he hastens to add, lest we means-test our giving—to the weddings of our kings. But we Christ followers, in our church services, can't be bothered to welcome in, sit next to and smell a homeless person. I don't use we as rhetorical slight of hand; I am talking about myself as well.

If our theology were reflective of The Kingdom, which is to say orthodox in a meaningful sense, would not our church body—racially, socioeconomically—better reflect our Savior's radical welcome? If our body isn't diverse, if our works are not abundantly present and apparently good but often hidden, tired and of little to negative value to outsiders, then the theological tree from which our fruit hangs is proved rotting.

∿

It was a broken home, and depression in response, that made me a seeker as a teen. I was looking for God and also for where the hot chicks hung out; there was one place in town that held plausible claim to both.

In that youth group, Christ, whose words and deeds I'd heard before, to no effect, was suddenly beautiful to me. I was cynical and suicidal but all was fresh then, after I prayed the prayer. *It was the first time I'd spoken to God as a person, which made it the first time I felt heard.*

That room remains a sanctuary in my mind, no matter what the evangelical church and that evangelical church have done in offense since. That room, a basketball court surfaced with carpet, walled by interior stucco, soundtracked by Our God is an Awesome God on an electric drumset, and all in my experience, finally slowed and shined. I remember, in the lollipop-orange stage lights, the dust particles floating, as beautiful to me as when I was four and first noticed them suspended like that and danced in them sunlit at dusk—Magic Hour, we call it in Hollywood.

I remember going home from that experience to my brothers playing Mortal Kombat II, one of our less violent past-times. I remember looking past my stepbrother's brass-post bed to the fatalities being performed on the screen, my mind so gauzed by beauty and love I couldn't see what had ever been or could ever again be attractive about this game. *It may be silly but it was not mundane; it was a shift in consciousness unanticipated by dogma.*

My religious experience is not yours but awe, beauty and interconnection are how we commonly experience the divine. If one's religion manifests largely in anger and exclusion, it may be that this is not born of a religious experience but a degradation of religion as tool, God as magistrate, to license hate. I must tell American evangelicalism it offers much hate, fear and shame to uphold its structures. I must tell a Reformed *church (evangelical adjacent) like ours that we're often complicit. I've seen this abuse of power and shame-wielding push more away from Christ, never to return, than I've seen our words, even the best of them, bring hurting people in. A few centuries in, we have the data on our American theology. Our tree offers more poison than nourishment. We must judge the tree lacking and change. I believe Scripture instructs us to do so.*

On scripture. "Inerrant" is a word too hollow, too coldly intellectual for the Bible to use of itself; it should be no surprise when the word contorts our minds into reading Genesis as a biology textbook, Romans as a hate-crime endorsement. "God-breathed" is poetry; as such it can melt your heart, drive you mad, and yes, save your soul.

For a long time I've been going deaf to arguments over a point of scripture, chapter and verse, if the church you allege holds the orthodoxy looks nothing like the Kingdom I see in Scripture. If the church in question is not radically welcoming, or if it lacks joy and love, you are but the clanging gong of Charlie Brown wah-wah-wahs in my ears. And so instead of engaging exclusion by exclusion to explain my rejection of the theology you've had every right to assume we shared to this point, I'll refer to Newbigin: "It is never legitimate to lift a particular piece out of the Bible and treat is as if it were in isolation 'the Word of God.'" That is an exultantly high view of Scripture; excising fragments, to be flung as shrapnel, is profanity.

~

I was always weird there in my youth group, and in every church since, always on the periphery even when leading, but I was accepted enough, far more than in my home. It was only my location in Scottsdale, Arizona and status as a young white man that let me find what I was looking for in the evangelical church. What if I'd been a weirdo and not white? How attractive are the evangelical youth groups in Detroit? No, "orthodox" theology is not a tablet carried down from the mountain; it is a construct and luxury of privilege, upheld by privilege, including my own.

But it has sunk in. The fear of being labeled apostate, even by myself, on any point of theology has kept me from an embrace of the marginalized, which I cannot believe is Christ's desire: "God is love," and I repent. I quote chapter and verse here only because I believe this is a scripture written to sum up the whole of Scripture and thus not a white lie when chosen. If we believe verses about the death penalty for sexuality are likewise summative, Lord have mercy, I say in prayer.

~

As a pastor caring for people who have been in church for years, shame has always been a concern for my work. Brené Browne here: guilt (I have done something wrong), interestingly, sometimes serves a positive function, motivating a person to change; shame (there is something wrong with who I am) is consistently maladaptive. In other words, if you're shamed over a behavior, like drinking, or cheating, or being racist, you won't stop, you'll double down on it. No matter the evil committed by the other, shame will not reform them. It will make you feel better for a bit, for a political moment, but it will harden and poison you too. In driving the other away and back into the behavior you despise, your hate will be re-re-rejustified.

Incidentally, I'm sorry if my words of correction here impact you as shaming. It isn't my intent and I know it won't achieve my ends. I've lived in shame my whole life. I can't imagine I've lost the language entirely. I apologize for that.

~

In the people I've had the pleasure to pastor and in my broader relationships, the American church is the most consistent institutional ally of shame I've encountered. This is not only morally wrong, it is, as it drives people away, killing the church. The church, by the numbers, is dying.

To be whole, we must stop shaming and being shamed. It sucks the color out of our lives, leaving only good and evil as categories, which erases empathy, which negates all but a selfish caricature of love.

To hold up one way of being born God's child as superior is to tell all others they are less than, other than. Evangelicals must believe sexuality and poverty, regardless of the data, are choices, in order to believe they are "loving the sinner, hating the sin," guilting and not shaming. But shame is the clear lived experience of these othered groups and a theology that doesn't listen and respond to lived experience is dying if not already dead. A theology that draws distinctions in power between men and women is inherently shaming (there is something wrong with who I am), no matter how limited in scope (preaching) it aims to be, as being a woman is not a choice; it is ineligible for guilt.

I can no longer stomach—it does indeed make me sick—the cognitive dissonance between the love we say our theology derives from and the shame it results in. I don't believe a theology that systematically shames can be right. On the other hand, a spiritual practice that flees from shaming and toward loving will cover a multitude of doctrinal agnosticisms, I believe.

Our denomination has no overtly racist theological tenants. But it doesn't directly address the othered conditioned of being a person of color in America—in the church. Medium is the message; authors are the audience. If nearly all of evangelical orthodoxy is penned and preached by old white men, such that even the ancient African fathers of the faith like Augustine and Athanasius have been white-washed and Anglicized in our seminaries, whose perspectives could this orthodoxy possibly reflect? Whose interests could it serve? If we continually stand on the sidelines on matters of civil rights, slower to change even than society as a whole, then our theology, in spirit, if not in letter, is a racist theology.

~

To state the obvious, white men are in the position of power in the American evangelical church. Generally, we haven't embraced the role of servant leader and lifted up other voices, as I believe Christ would have us do. Feeling disempowered elsewhere, we have clung to and abused power in the church. That power is subverting God's will and contorting His image—can we not, looking upon the pharisaical hypocrisy our theology has wrought—admit the *wreck? Our leaders mocked the first black president's faith, no matter the fruit of it in his marriage and family, no matter the credibility of his conversion story and church community involvement. The same leaders hold up the next, white supremacist sympathizer, serial adulterer, serial liar, who has said he doesn't confess his sins to God, as both believing and unassailable. None of these leaders pastored our church. But nor has our church condemned their words, ever. Complicity is a tumor I want to excise, from myself at least.*

If we white American Christians call this wreck by its name, then it is our duty to question our own power. It is time for white men in the pastorate and elsewhere to sit down and start listening.

For me, at long last, this means leaving the pulpit and resigning from our denomination. I don't believe an institution can change unless its primary beneficiaries act.

∼

Family, writing this, thinking about leaving, was deeply destabilizing and I am scared. I don't think all, or maybe even most, others like me should make the same decision. But I do believe that white Christians must confront our complicity—complicity being the passive form of hate—in this toxic culture. And act.

I don't pretend to know the three steps to achieve that but I do suggest one thing we can do is say no to shame and any system that manufactures it. I don't know which factories can be rebuilt by existing staff, which need a complete overhaul and which must be abandoned. Some are so hazardous they require demolition.

I am sorry I wasn't a better leader. I'm sorry this all got pushed down into my gut to be heaved up all at once. I'm sorry I'm leaving. But I can't, in good conscious, stay. I love you and I wish you and you all the best.

∼

I said "Let us pray." When the congregation bowed, I thought, *I should just run out the side door now.* But I stayed. By the coffee and donuts, I shook hands as people said their goodbyes. No one argued with me, took a swing at me, or physically removed me from the pulpit. I can think of at least thirty people who would've liked to; they've cornered me at Christmas parties. George, I remember well, an aerospace engineer who designed smart bombs, and then drones, which I imagine you, Father, view as utterly consistent with the Christ you follow. And maybe it is. Maybe it is a different Christ we've been talking about all this time.

But George and his conservative faction, the faction that gives an outsized tithe and so has outsized influence, it is a political righteousness they've been holding me to, some metastasized definition of pro-life with no life in it. I, and other pastors like me, have allowed them to hold us to their theological litmus tests with the ever-present threat that if we stepped out of line in the pulpit, they'd take their (money) ball and go home, one or two of their ilk dropping off, or at least *calling a meeting,* every time *social justice* rang from the pulpit. It's a ransom I can no longer abide.

If the you of ten years ago had been there, I believe you would have shouted me down during that sermon. These days, I know you are more weary, more defeated by perceived cultural losses and actual relational ones; I imagine you would have just stared me down, perhaps walked out down the center aisle in a show of your disdain, as I was preaching. If you've read the whole thing without tearing this up, I thank you for your endurance.

I thought Steve would mount some public show of disapproval but he waited until the post-service crowd had thinned to almost nothing before summoning me with a wave toward the back door of the building. He was surprisingly charitable. "Johnny," he said to me, in his practiced fatherly way, "perhaps you were John the Baptist come to speak truth to power," before informing me I wouldn't be preaching the remaining services that day.

4

Living Room

I AM THINKING OF those Saturday mornings, dusted sunlight pouring in through the bay window of the aging craftsman on Kensington Road. Dust again glues a memory to the sublime. I wonder if I am ever slowed enough, concentrated enough, to see it, except when enraptured.

We would gather, twenty, then thirty, eventually forty of us, in that large-for-LA living room. The house creaking, perpetually unsettled, on a hill overlooking a green ravine between it and the next and next and next hills in Echo Park, the wild poinsettias tall, looping and lopping as Dr. Seuss trees. The thought of that home, our meeting place, is all flowers blooming, eternally spring, my wife Leah's allergies eternal, hardwood floors the plank-width and finish of a bowling lane, full, always full, fullest in the all-corners kitchen next to the shitty pretty antique stove, music and conversation, shouts, songs, prayers of blessing and, in the many evening gatherings there—we couldn't get enough of one another—beeeeeeer.

I remember one of those parties I stepped behind the drumset myself, played along with what lineup was rotated in, the surprised smiles of the artists around me saying *one of us*, I dared to think. Nate, a pianist, able to do just that because he tours with bigger acts, plays in churches, and records with whoever, and Salt, a street artist and caterer, lived in that house together for years. It was shortly after I started pastoring the subchurch there that Leah and I were married, all in the community attending the wedding, blessing the marriage. A year into our marriage we got to move into the Kensington house ourselves and replace their subletter.

Blessing. A hard concept for me, even before I left my church and wife. Perhaps one day I'll be evolved enough to frame the end of my marriage as, and believe it is, something neutral: a dissolution, an ending, out of my hands, or at least held by others too. But for now the shame all points in my direction. Perhaps not the blame; I feel myself test-piloting some of that toward you and yours, toward God himself. But my operant emotional reality is that I left her; I won't mince words otherwise until it feels otherwise.

But blessing. So often prayers seemed to me a strained bestowing of holiness on a thing, a hollow naming that didn't make it so. But that day's blessings weren't hollow. They acknowledged the holiest thing I'd tasted: communion, with my wife, with those *brothers and sisters*, the blessing a naming of the thing that deepened the thing, a prayer of thanks for the fact and a prayer of petition to enlarge the fact.

My hands shake as I think of Leah in that home, a trembling of longing for the most vivid memories I've got, and aching that they might be unremembered—because they can't be held, just surveyed, photos of The White City before it was dismantled, bolted to a gallery wall.

Our honeymoon was there; Salt and Nate vacated for ten days. Ten days that humming hub that weekly housed all thirty hearts by that time, singing for one another and for God, housed only us, fucking. In every room, no visitors please, fucking especially in the living room, next to Nate's Hammond Organ, upon which Be Thou My Vision was played, practiced, played, practiced, fucking on top of the blankets and pillows that served as backup modesty coverings for the women, sitting in circle, as the men sat across, as we read, verse by turn-taking verse, The Word of God.

Sexual shame wasn't a part of our life then. It had been a part of Leah's past. But we were abstinent until marriage and so (I believed in magic) the shame was exorcised. The shame was on pause, I guess I've come to believe. Perhaps we willed the pause, so desperate were we to be born again into a marriage as we were into a faith, desperate to believe a single extravagant act—Praying the Prayer or Saying the Vows—could wash us clean.

5

Starting Out in the Afternoon

I'M RUNNING NOW, I know. I have my reasons. I hope some are good. I still need to believe I am a good man, even if I no longer know who I'd trust to bestow this judgment, even if I'm disgusted by my neediness.

I can't let myself off the hook. Even if I'm beginning to wonder if my pastors, self, you, Father, made up the hook.

The end of my marriage will be official within weeks. I just didn't have the strength to wait in Los Angeles for it. This Presbyterian longsuffering is dead in me. I am hoping the word *goodbye* will grow in me while I'm away so I can return to Leah, package in hand.

We church people talk about marriage, children, belief in Calvin's double predestination, any hard thing, as though it must be lived up to. As though the hard way isn't just the best, it's the only. As though life is a fight. Whether I believe that anymore, I don't know. But I'm experimenting with the premise that it's not just fight or be defeated, that there's a third way— escape. Escapist! rings the charge in my ears, as I nod affably in agreement, in rhythm with the sounds of Neutral Milk Hotel sputtering out the half-blown speakers of my '92 Volvo 850.

I'm driving north, for now, meandering up the Pacific Coast Highway, as one does when one has nowhere to be, when one is white in LA, when one's midlife crisis hits early. This album was still a pet secret even among the cool kids when it was passed to me, in hard copy, like an out-of-print text from a persecuted religious sect, by the artists I somehow found myself next to in college. Northwestern, so far from all I'd known, any music I could have come to know, in Arizona. Listening to it made me want to add art to my life and to my future preaching, made me migrate to WNUR, the college radio station, to discover and play more of this. It is alarming music, alarmed me then, waking me to the possibility of a screaming and trembling hunger for God, mouthed alongside mourning for the worst in us, alongside lust for the flesh, all jumbled, a mess alright with its own mess, unshapable into category and doctrine. It became *worship music* for me then, helping me reframe spirituality for myself, and for others in my care, at Reformed University Fellowship and beyond. The secret is long out; what was protected cool-kid music is now self-conscious I-was-cool music for those of us aging out of making the scene, music well-known now even in a Christian people group like the subchurch. And I don't care that it's no longer a secret; it still plays the same notes on me.

As I drive away, I don't know what in me it's stirring. This is the first time I've listened to this music in years. I wasn't in the market for any more alarm than my experience was silent-alarming in me.

6

Away

AWAY FROM LOS ANGELES, where I'd been almost fifteen years, after college in Chicago and through seminary, through thirteen years of work for one church where I would never, could never—it became clear—make it past associate pastor status, preaching my handful of Sundays a year, past scraping by month to month and year to year, past being just outside the centers of power. As much as I always talked about following the most humble leader, especially with you, Father, I admit that being left out of power was devastating for me. I had to pretend it wasn't because, philosophically, I didn't think it should be; interpersonally, I couldn't give you the satisfaction of mirroring your disappointment in me. Not in front of you, at least.

The truth is I wanted that power the whole damn time. You tell yourself that power within the church doesn't count because, really, attaining that power would just represent a more effective station from which to exercise your humility. Ha. What laughable intellectual gymnastics that is to me now, as is much of our theology, and yet how long it went uninterrogated by me.

But I took my faith seriously. Whatever our disagreements, I imagine you'd acknowledge as much. That's how I saw my gadfly status at the time: seriousness. As such, I regularly questioned how down with running the church as a business JC would be—yes, while still trying to make my income within it (to work for a church is to constantly balance one cognitive dissonance against another). I don't believe this oft-stated objection, or my tallying the Mercedeses in the parking lot at Sunday services, helped my professional mobility. I just couldn't quite figure how to claim Christ and subtract the idealism, add the materialism.

I was put in charge of pastoring the community of artists—we had brilliant ones. In our conversations, I let you minimize this work unchallenged and I'm sorry for that. I was made for that work; I loved that work. I knew it was a way to push me outside the circles of power and money in the church, out with the weird and desperate whose grittier problems the pastors had no idea how to pastor, but I was still happy, mostly. Able to feel my faith was real among them, feel, a little longer, it was less than mostly hypocrisy. That ministry extended my lifespan within the church maybe another four years.

I may be questioning everything now, but I can't imagine questioning the value of that time. Should it all prove false, those times were true, I believe still, balls to bones.

II

7

Ventura

I STOP FOR GAS in Ventura. I go in to get coffee and the best looking thing on the rolling grill, a taquito of girth exceeding even the jumbo hotdogs, which I regret in every stage of choosing, paying 3.28 for, consuming and digesting. The dude at the register has tattoo sleeves and methed out teeth. He doesn't currently look hollow or high and the evangelical in me, which I realize I may never eradicate, thinks *good for him*. That thought moves quickly out of my mind and I'm left wondering: was he once, in his thought system, his community, his addiction, as convinced as I that the path he was on was the only, the predestined, one? There are so many ways to be in the wide world, which is somehow a revelation to me; in my life of contemplation and study I somehow never spent much time thinking of it. Now every person I meet is a chasm of curiosities. He catches me staring.

"Thanks," I tell him.

He nods back, accusingly, and I can't just keep walking like humans do.

"Sorry," I say. "I'm . . . going through something, and I find myself—"

"Come again," he says, his eyes jagged, his forearm veins awakened by his clenched fists. I nod and go.

"Forgive me," I say, after the door has shut behind me. The line between prayer and thought is fading for me now, a mostly beautiful thing, as well as the line between audible and inaudible, apparently, which is of some concern.

"What?" A black woman in her mid-twenties is on her way in as my mumbling gives her pause.

"Nothing. Sorry, talking to myself." Her guard softens immediately, my contrition helping us each out of the fretting fear that I am insane or harassing. Her teeth are crooked and beautiful. She is about the same age as most of my friends, the people formerly in my charge at church, but she looks impossibly young to me; I see no worry on her. Her arm tattoos, and especially her chest tattoo, are dense and intricate. I want to see them but her skin is too dark to tell much from a nonintrusive distance and gaze. How much less intimate are tattoos on people of my complexion.

Her hair is in narrow, shoulder-length dreads. She dresses like young dressed when I was young, all black hoodie and safety pins and band buttons, bands from before even my time, curated as a shout-out to the institution of band-buttons—Fugazi, Pavement and, dear God, that old-timey painting of a bathing lady and her son, waving a hello from the beach, a drumhead covering her face, the cover art for In the Aeroplane Over the Sea by Neutral Milk Hotel. There are also buttons for Naz, Lauren Hill, Talib Kweli, the rap I never listened to but got told to often enough I felt guilty about it.

"What are you doing tonight," she asks. It's not a come-on, I don't think. Not that I know, after this long in the church and in shame, what a come-on looks like. And anyway, I make some kind of defensive show as I raise my hand, thumbing my wedding-ringed finger, although I have left the church and my wife.

She waves her hand dismissively. "Not like that. There's a party. I'm Janey. At the loft."

8

Living Room, Living Room

ON THOSE SUBCHURCH SATURDAYS we'd make a big breakfast, sing the old hymns and read the Psalms or a gospel together. It started when the economy was still bad, when the church capped my paid hours at twenty, whatever my actual hours were. We were all desperate, desperate to get our work outside of ourselves and into the world, desperate for connection— these artists had always been double-weirdos—looked upon with suspicion by both their creative and faith communities, which before this moment had never co-existed. The magic of looking around that room and seeing men and women he respected as both artists and people of faith, Salt told me, tears in his stoic eyes, was a miracle to him. He told me this as a good-bye when I left the subchurch, I think as a way of saying "thanks for the mem'ries. I'll try not to blame you like the rest do."

I was as desperate as my artist friends, still running from my mother's hot addictions and your cold legalisms, Father, from Scottsdale to Chicago, the far edge of the country for a westerner like me, New York being too alien to even be a part of my map of possibilities, and finally to be a preacher in LA, of what gospel I don't now know. If I didn't then either, I did at least have a sense of purpose in leading and being taught by that subchurch, which, I see now, was more a church than any any of us had ever had.

It was the Psalms that brought us together, the Psalms of Lament in particular. They gave voice to our sadness, anger and pain, which our churches had not. These psalms get forgotten, thanksgiving and praise be-ing the expressions of the human condition the church is comfy with. Even if, theologically, we reject the Prosperity Gospel as the funhouse mirror of Christian faith it is, it has still burrowed under the skin of us in the American church, found its way to dementing the heart of what we secretly believe faith is for: success. *Success*. I hear the sibilance here echoing off my skull walls, as though the serpent himself spoke it, if not in The Garden, in my garden, the fruit I shoulda kept my sticky desires away from.

The Psalms of Lament get dark. Structurally, they almost all have a redemptive turn, after descending into the muck and wallowing in it, at least one sunny moment at the end, something like, "But I know the Lord will deliver his people."

Psalm 88 is different. The Psalms are in the middle of the bible, 150 chapters long. Psalm 88 starts in the muck and stays there, ending "darkness is my only friend." This expression of unrelenting grief and anger with God is in the heart of the heart of the Bible, which I took to mean that God can handle us at our messiest; He gave us the script. In writing that, I'm aware of how *put together* your habits with God are. How I wish I believed my musings here could shift your perspective, ever, about anything. Let alone about faith.

A minister can be like an artist. The power we give preaching in the church, the opportunity to hold a thousand people in your thrall, your words and God's Word at least intermingled, confusable for one another if not the same, isn't unlike what the actors I knew wanted: to speak their truth. Their foolishness was no more foolish than mine, the culmination of their dream only somewhat less likely (seminaries churn out baristas about as efficiently as drama schools do), and perhaps more beautiful for the brokenness they wore on their sleeves. We ministers hide ours way down, a rock in the gut.

My professional and personal life may have just now come apart, dragged down into this gaping doubt and rage in me, but it has been growing for years, three at least. When you buy in as fully as I had, working for the church, worshiping in the church, marrying in the church, having your friends in the church, then bringing your friends and your worship under your roof, to let go of your job is to let go of everything—you've let them all down, you see—and you can't crawl back from that without pushing some rocks up hills. And the rocks, like the fighting, I have given up. Perhaps your church-hopping, predicated upon a doctrinal purity none can measure up to, is self-protective. Perhaps anyone who dives in as deeply as I did is bound for a deconstruction at some point, when the theology of the body of Christ and the facts of any actual body finally fall out of the tension they've hung in, overlong.

Through all this, my marriage felt different, bonded by something or things beyond all the rest, my wife ready and willing to stick. But today my marriage feels taken away, withdrawn by God the Father, proven as withholding as you, my earthly father. This vacillation toward blaming you is troubling. I know it's a fleeting respite. I naturally look inward for my hate. That's the home base I know I'll return to.

9

Julia of West LA

THERE WAS SOME FINITE number of fights I had in me, I think, some unknown but exact duration of dogma I could endure.

Julia, an ex-girlfriend of mine from the beginning of my time in LA,
was a part of the subchurch the last fifteen months of her life. She was an
actress, a beautiful, talented and unsuccessful one, who had contracted an
aggressive form of cancer. She'd been living the isolating life of professional
failure in West LA, and couldn't handle that with this. She would sit with
us and listen to our prayers, a bad job or a desire for a relationship, with
such care and curiosity, before asking God that no more of her reproductive
organs be cut out, please.

She called me because she wanted to find a community to be a part
of and, I found out, a faith strong enough to cure her. That was what the
churches she had run to and from, to and from, had all taught her, that
any failing in her was a failure, of faith. I've always imagined this is how
you think of me, Father, a professional failure because I am a spiritual one.
I certainly internalized that. I want to be fair, it may not have been from
you, or you alone, but from some other failed father figure in the church,
God knows there are dozens of candidates in my patriarchy. What strange
twists life has taken. My turn toward evangelicalism was a rebellion against
you at the time, your religion then nothing but a broad Judeo-Christian
moralism. The God of the Prodigal Son was all that I—longing for your
embrace—needed then. Evangelicalism then gave me the categories of patriarchal authoritarianism that sent me seeking, always, to *honor* you, seeking relationship no matter your terms, no matter your actions. You were

then attracted to the evangelical faith, a much cleaner fit than I, able then to actively exploit our now-shared categories. And so somehow, misunderstanding me throughout my life, pushing me away, shaming me, you've maintained authority over me. Quite the trick, in which I volunteered as your assistant.

In fifteen months, I couldn't issue enough "it's not your faults" to have Julia look at me, at 85 pounds, sallow and pale as Christ in the tomb, any way other than with a blanketing and contrite shame: "Thank you for saying that, but where's the penance?" I was, glad for her sake, I wasn't a Catholic priest.

But I believe she heard my words as a dismissal. Giving her that penance would have been the greater mercy.

She was so afraid to die, so unlike whatever the blurry picture of a saint in pain was in my mind. I was at her hospital bed, I remember, the worst hospital of all she'd been in, one that was exclusively for end-of-life care, which hospitals, I am told, are generally the shittiest. I was sitting there waiting for her to wake, praying for her yet again. She woke gently and calmly, for once. I got close and she said my name, smiling, hushed and low, a breathy wavering whisper of "John" like the beginning of a 70s folk song. It was ten seconds before the pain repossessed her and she was catapulted away from me, screaming, clutching at my hands, begging Christ, begging me, the nurses, the walls.

She never let her faith come off as anything but desperate and it was more beautiful for that, the cross no adornment on her but a cross indeed, a marker and instrument of passion.

I remember one night, in her West LA apartment, where she'd been, rent-controlled for fifteen years, the water damage on the drywall like veins, the veins like throbbing as we prayed, circled around her in her living room for hours. The cancer was everywhere, past the point where pragmatists would say there's any chance, past the point where Presbyterians truly believed there was, at the point where the charismatics are surer than ever that just the right prayer, the most accurate faith, would surely save. Julia came from the charismatics.

We were a motley bunch. Although I was ordained by the Presbyterians, the subchurch drew in strays from all over the church world, I think because all stripes of the faith have trouble with artists, artists being committed to exploration and exploration being an antagonist of dogma. Because of our varied theological backgrounds group prayer was always a wild ride.

As we huddled and prayed for Julia that night, a new guy, Rance, said, "Lord, give Julia faith to move mountains."

I tapped him on the shoulder and gave him eye contact I pray he correctly interpreted as "Fuck you, Rance." Of all the horrid skills the American church has perfected, faith-shaming the sick is one of the darkest.

Each of Julia's doctors, on separate occasions, who had all seen dozens of humans slowly scooped out to empty by this death, volunteered that they'd never seen anyone suffer as hard or as long as Julia. Their voices were hushed, their lips pursed, choosing the damn language of comfort to convey it. Did they think we thought she was faking it? The bowels-deep moans like birthing, for days on end, interrupted three hours out of twenty-four, when the four opiates she was on were at their combined maximum strength and she slept, slept always with nightmares, guilty nightmares of all she thought she'd failed.

We had a young church, a younger subchurch, and I was not the preacher of first choice for most. So hers was only the third funeral I preached and the first for a friend. She asked me to share the gospel, as her *seeker* friends from her show business endeavors would be there. And I did. It felt like a betrayal, this slow-played altar call. I certainly still believed then that Christ saves, may still, but this unsettled me deeply and I know why now: her life was the only *witness* worth hearing.

The gall, to stand there and interpret her life into a meaning beyond itself, which was beautiful, and broken to shattering, anxious to trembling, and unremittingly kind. But she asked me to have the gall. And you try saying *no* to Christ in the tomb.

After Julia's death, I had another couple years of ardent church work left in me. But looking back, that distilling a life into a sermon was a crassness I never recovered from, an emblem for the way we in the church can take the most faithful and beautiful thing—suffering well, ending well, never calling the pain and the doubt by other names, never falsely turning to praise when the faithful thing is to stay in lament—and just reshape it into a means to another, crasser, end.

10

But Ventura

THE LOFT IS AN old airplane hangar, a Bohemian dream—of artist *coliving* and collaboration. Drywall and less permanent partitions have been thrown up to divide chunks of the space into artists' studios and quarters.

"Twenty of us live here full-time. Another thirty have their studios here," Janey says, parental pride beaming.

"You put this all together," I ask.

"We all did. I'm the creative director, so I guess I wrangled a lot of cats."

"You herd cats."

"What" she asks, as I wince.

"Sorry, I care too much about words." She smiles wryly, enjoying my self-deprecation.

I find myself wishing there were some other me, perhaps who'd never set foot in a church, who could unguardedly enjoy being enjoyed. Janey walks me on. She says her hellos as we pass by a bunch of the others. She doesn't introduce me. This stands out to me, I think because hospitality is such a self-conscious value for my people that I don't have a rubric for bringing someone to a party without formal introductions all night long. I realize my cultural bias, remind myself not to be offended and enjoy the anonymity.

The Loft must be over half a football field long, just a few miles inland from the beach. The kind of thing we in the subchurch were always dying for—never enough space in LA, never enough money to pay the rent on a place to live and work, never enough time to be together for all of us, flung about town, needing to commute for community. I can't decide if it's more likely that Janey and her friends are squatting here or that someone's dad owns it. My jaw is dropped open.

"It's home," she says. "Beer?"

She walks me to the beer tubs in the middle of the space and grabs me a Ventura County IPA. They buy fancy beer here and yet Pabst Blue Ribbon fills the majority of the tubs. Is there a PBR rule among artists, which extends at least past the LA County line?

"What's your medium," she asks.

"I'm not an artist."

"Words. You a writer?"

I stare at her for what feels like a minute. "I was a pastor. I don't know what I am now."

"Like a priest?"

I shrug and cringe.

She laughs.

"Except you can have a wife," she says, pointing at my ring.

I just nod.

Janey has taken me back outside, toward the fire pit, around which a dozen people are sitting. They pass around bongs. This is the first custom at this party that's different enough from our own to make me flinch a bit, reflexively, defensively, as it comes up against the bubble, the invisible shield of long-held rules, around me. Once I calm myself down, ask myself what it is I really think, versus what I was taught decades ago by fearsome and fearful legalists, the bongs are a curiosity to me (I'm well aware some of my flock smoked and vaped and oiled, just in private [decorum is a high value for us Christ followers, somehow, despite his complete lack of it]). I think a moment on this, wondering, as it is legal and doesn't assault your liver, if this custom is really any worse than drinking. The wondering has me feeling open-minded and generous of spirit, and then downright magnanimous as I decide that no, I ought not presume pot's moral inferiority to beer.

"Bump," asks a dude next to me. I don't know what he's talking about but I turn to see he's sprung out cocaine or some white powder, in lines on a mirror.

I feel my cheeks blush at the realization and am glad for the cover of low firelight.

Janey peers at me with a crooked smile.

"No thank you," I manage.

I do have three beers though, which I've heard from no less than five Presbyterian pastors is their public maximum as well. Three is a special number of beers for me, specialer for the booziness of the IPAs, where I feel more myself, warm and full—of the spirit, I want to say, a feeling I associate with fellowship at subchurch parties, and so also with prayer, even if silent, and song, even if not *worship*. Three beers gives me the feeling I understand what those monks, chanting prayers and brewing and drinking, chanting prayers and brewing and drinking, have been at all these centuries.

11

Birthday Party

NOVEMBER 8, 2016 WAS my thirty-fifth birthday and election day. As my wife and I walked the three blocks to our polling place, down the tree-root exploded sidewalks of Angelino Heights, the sun was warm and the day was clear. We smiled and laughed more than we had in weeks, a nervous laughter that gave way to a childish one, all fart jokes and puns. We were so happy and sure to be done with the election, done with Trump. It isn't that we thought of Hillary as a hero, Father—our heroes are less into war—just a non-clown. Leah let me pendulum swing our hands back and forth in time with our steps, our fingers interlaced, childlike in a way she usually put a stop to. I carried her small body piggyback the last block. Since I left, I know I view all my memories of her through rose- or shit-colored lenses but that morning with her was and is beautiful, I believe.

It's a walking neighborhood and the anxiety had been palpable, in people's nervous gates and twitchy vapes, for months. But that morning all of Echo Park seemed to hum, my people who'd been there for years still able to afford it with rent control or bunkbeds or the occasional professional success and the new people too—the TV writers and design firm owners.

Watching the election cycle within the American church, even from the vantage of one like ours, which didn't (mostly!) vote Trump, had us worn down, tired and sad. It was a great surprise to us that swathes of the American church could go in, exuberantly, for this gaping orange maw of micropornographies and macroresentments. We had been apologizing on behalf of all Christians for the year this Christian-Trump entanglement had existed, somehow put in the position of having to argue Christianity can be a way of love, forgiveness, and peace. This was exhausting work. It exhausts me further, which exhaustion I apologize to you for, Father, to know so well your own disagreements with me on all this, your pity for my naiveté. This pity makes me sad more than angry.

We gathered at our polling place with our artists' community and voted. I remember Glenda, the four-year-old daughter of Jimmy and Jessica, coming out of the voting booth yelling, "I voted for the first girl!" We all laughed and smiled easily at coffee afterwards, sure that she had.

"I'm so done with it," Jimmy said to me, hungrily slurping his coffee. "Politics. Twitter. Maybe church. I need a break for forever."

"It'll look better tomorrow," I told him. I put an arm around him and smiled warmly, coercively, until finally he mirrored my smile. I know I meant what I said, but I also see in it what I see in so much of my church work only now. I thought I was different from the platitude offerers, that I ministered and counseled with patience. I see I was unable to sit with people in pain, to minister with their guilt or doubt, ministering at them instead. Maybe I could linger there, in the unresolved, a bit longer than my peers but I too wanted to skip ahead to the resolution, which in this case was a rouse: no resolution was coming. "It's always darkest before the dawn," I might as well have told him. Unless the Lord blots out the sun.

For my birthday, Leah had arranged a day for me with my closest friends. We went hiking along the ocean, Corral Canyon out in Malibu. That day's physical beauty was mixed up in this great relief, a relaxing of tension in the jaw, because it was all over—Nate Silver and the New York Times promised—and we could begin to mend, begin even to reconcile.

At night, we were back in Echo Park at Sunset Beer where they were projecting CNN's coverage. I left my own birthday party at 8pm as the coverage took a turn, had to walk back home to be away from it and with my wife.

I love those three men, my tiny birthday party group, very much. Praying, struggling through the Bible, cultivating spiritual disciplines of self-denial and depth of thought, together for years, had bonded us tightly. I know that bond hasn't gone away for me; I don't question the value of what we did, just some of the presuppositions it sat on top of. I hope they still feel bonded to me. Well, two of them. In the case of Ryan, I know he doesn't.

I abruptly left serving the subchurch a few months ago. I broke down, just couldn't do it anymore. I know that businessmen and church leaders such as yourself don't understand the word "couldn't" in this context but I'd hoped artists would. Diana, a member of the subchurch, threw a party during that time; she was kind enough to invite me; I was foolish enough to accept. When I arrived, Ryan was a few beers in—you're probably beginning to see this is possibly the entire attraction of our denomination—orthodoxy, yes, but with a love of intellectualism, literature, and beer. He got me in a corner, locked his sad child's eyes on me and said "Why'd you leave us?" his voice quivering in the middle. I almost laughed, it was so on-the-nose, the nose of my worst fears of who I am and the effects of what I'd done. To regain his vocal footing, he raised his voice so *leave us* was loud enough for ten people to hear, and stare, drawing the stares of most everyone there. I told him I was sorry and left the party.

12

And Ventura

AT AROUND ONE, I'M standing with thirty people in a corner of the hangar listening to a singer-songwriter, something sparse of image and instrumentation about the Arizona Desert through a California rear view: "A train for the desert is leaving/ like a man swimming straight out to see/ I left you on your porch in the evening/ like the dew leaves the moss on the tree." The man is howling his song, sweat pouring down, his voice quivering from an excess of strength, not a lack. I am up in my head, anguishing over his lostness and his pain, over how *unsaved* he must be. This hollow thought is just habit; it is self-justification paid for by judgment of the other. I never believed I should be judging like that but I did it anyway; I can only see it now in the light of the detritus of the judgment that proves the judgment: the still-there category of savedness.

But the truth is there's no one in this airplane-sized room as lost as me.

And so the singer has me crying for myself. And/or the beers do. And/or the leaving of my wife and church. By the time he's singing about being as big as the ocean for her, of finally being called magnificent by her, I am weeping and then gurgling, sending the closest people to my right and left inching away, which is of course when Janey inches toward and takes my hand. I reflexively pull away but she holds my hand tight. I squirm to gain distance from the scene but she pulls me back to my spot.

"Stay and listen," she says. And I do.

∽

"Do you have somewhere to stay tonight," Janey asks.

41

"No plans, but . . ."

"Stay with us," she says.

I look at her, trying to wait her out, get her to speak next.

"There's a couch," she says, mercifully attending to whatever it is I still believe about purity, sex, my marriage.

She settles me in to the couch, spreading a blanket over me. No one has done this for me since my mother, when I was a sick child, which I was so often. As her hand moves above my chest, I see the whole tattoo on it, wild flowers growing out of plated desert mud. I touch her hand, which stills us both, and is the most intimacy I can stand.

I sleep on the couch, she in the chair next to me, stroking my hair as I fall asleep, dreaming instantly, sleeping deeper than shallow from the start, never deeper than the anxiety of dreams, in which the Volvo is falling apart. The brakes are failing over and over, on a mountain road down into a ditch, on the PCH down a cliff side, in LA swerving to avoid foodcarts, children, my congregants from the subchurch.

∼

In the morning I am fed a poptart by Jake, a commune member who sleeps one church rec room partition over. Janey brings me coffee and asks if I have left my wife and I say yes, weeping easily, gurgleless. Janey works as a new therapist, a trainee. She says that leaving my job and my church and my community and my wife makes this a time of profound destabilization and that I should be staying with a friend, which would provide a sense of continuity and a home base.

"I've left my friends," I say. "They don't want me."

"How do you know that's true," she asks. "I imagine you have kind friends."

"*Charitable.*"

"Sure," she says.

I just shake my head.

She reaches out for my hand. I manage to pull it away before she can touch me.

"Have you ever heard of self-compassion," she asks. "It circles back into compassion for others and around again."

I don't tell her that this is the least attractive concept.

13

Blue Bunny

THERE IS A PHOTO of me; I'm about six, in a tiny Sunday golf-shirt, cuddling a bright blue bunny. I don't know if you remember this photo, as it had been with my mother since the divorce, one relic I recovered from her house after her death. I am looking directly at the camera, which is held by my mother, and I have the most adult sad smile, this closed-lipped flinch of compassion fatigue. You would be together another five years, when a *comfortable* life would come unglued. We would live in wealth until then; I wouldn't be fully parentified by Mom until then. But it is hard to look in my bunny-blue eyes without thinking *kid sees it coming*.

14

And Ventura

SALT CALLS ME. HE'S been calling me and texting me, as have others, whom I've muted with impunity.

"Sorry, man."

"What you sorry for," he asks, a kind reproach in his voice, like I'm crazy to admit the damage I've done, some of which he's been the victim of.

"I'm sorry I haven't picked up but it's a hard time."

"I can't imagine," he says. "I'm available."

"I don't think talking would help."

"Why?"

"Pffft," is my best transcription of the fart noise that comes out of me. After sighing histrionically a number of times, I let my still-felt obligation to Salt pipe me up.

"I talked for many years, vigilantly defending my actions and beliefs. But I don't want to do that with people who *know* my actions are indefensible."

"I don't believe that."

"And you're the only person I've picked up for."

"Your talk won't hurt me."

There is a long silence. His be-the-good-friend stance is exhausting me.

"Leah's parents are here at the house," he says. "They—"

"Fuck, man."

"I'm sorry," he says. "I didn't know what was the right thing. For her. For you."

I lose it, crying angrily.

"Please don't fucking talk about the right thing and her. I can't come home. Okay?"

"Okay, you're right," he says. "I'm sorry. That I have no idea how to help."

"You don't need to tell them. I'm sorry they're putting that on you. But I *cannot.*"

"Okay. I understand," he says.

"Thank you."

"You can call me. I'm not gonna pressure you. Again. I'll be here."

"I really don't have the energy to explain myself, definitely not to them, definitely not now."

Janey calls for me from over my shoulder.

"Boys are going shooting," she says. I turn to see Jake, holding an assault rifle in his poptart hand. Behind him are three other dudes, putting pistols into a Hello Kitty backpack, filthy with gun oil stains, ammunition in a backpack from some other childhood.

"Goodbye, Salt," I say.

15

Violence

I HAVE THIS RECURRING nightmare. It stars you or my stepfather, Wayne, or my brother, James. You're coming at me across a large room. I yell *stop* if my words work that night, stretch my arms and hands and fingers out in desperate *stop* gestures, every night, boxer-shuffling backward but you keep coming at me. I shout please, yell angry, beg. I put my dukes up and bob my head to defend against your strikes and you keep coming at me. Until I'm backed against the wall when finally, to reluctantly save myself from your wild attack—there's no discipline in it, even when it's Wayne, master martial artist—I pop you in the face, just to back you off me. Most nights I get you on the button, your nose spurting blood as you go to the floor, at which point I find relief that it's over, that I've defused you, then guilt that I hurt you. But you get to your feet, wilder yet, and you keep coming at me. And the whole cycle repeats. No matter how I run or beg or defend, you won't rest, you won't stop attacking, and so I keep begging and crying and fighting, saving myself last moment after last moment, until you are a bloody clump and I realize, with a hollow in my gut I realize, you won't stop coming at me until I've beaten you to death.

I've never gotten there, where I've finally been forced to destroy you rather than be destroyed. I wake up, every time, shortly after the moment when I see the grim truth, in your zombied walk, zombied thrashing, zombied eyes, of your inexorability.

16

Desert Ghosts

"I GREW UP AROUND guns," I say—to prove what—from the back of the conversion van, captain's chairs and SDTVs dotting the interior, late 90s Chevy in pearl and green, hurtling toward the desert. "I just have been devoted to nonviolence. Which has meant not using guns. To me." These words sound to me like the stupidest possible combination of words in English, 18th century and forward.

"Why are you with us now," Jake asks.

"Where you come from," asks Paolo, the driver. Paolo is the only black person other than Janey I've seen since coming to The Loft.

"Well, I think I'm still non-violent. It's just . . . there were a lot of other rules . . . I'm starting to question which rules I need. Maybe target shooting isn't some moral violation. I come from L.A., Paolo."

"You know why we have these around?" Jake has a gleam in his eye as he picks up a banana clip duct-taped upside down to another banana clip. These do not, I am aware, comply with California's ban on high capacity magazines. I don't venture to ask whether his were grandfathered in.

"Coyotes," I ask, somehow feeling bold enough to joke with the gun person.

"Revolution," Jake says.

"Cooool," I say.

The plan is to destroy a car, Ray's old Chevy Impala, which he drives behind us in caravan. It will be filmed and made into a music video for Jake's band. I am doubtful about the prospects of this, aesthetically.

～

I'm happy there's a .45 automatic in the piñata of pistols. That was always my favorite gun for target shooting with my stepfather, Wayne. He gave it to me years ago when I moved to L.A. I've been meaning to return it to him for almost as many years because I became a pacifist and, for a year now, because I don't want this gun from that man anymore. You knew of our shooting, I remember, disapproved of it. Remember, Father, a time when as a conservative Christian, you didn't like guns, and my stepfather, owner of mere pistols, was defined as the gun nut? James tells me—I suppose your common conservatism made him a safe space for this fact—that you now own an AR-15. Its pretensions of absolutism aside, American Conservative Christianity is a moving target, it seems. I intend the shit out of that pun.

Shooting trips were impromptu ones, always coming out of nowhere from my stepfather, like when he'd roll up on my school and pull me out of class to see the new Schwarzenegger movie, his alcoholic lane drifting yet more pronounced on the shooting days.

As we walk out and place old bottles and cans against a berm, Ray offers me peyote. "I started this morning. Catch up."

I decline. Jake offers me cocaine and I decline. Paolo remains aloof, drinking from a fifth of Bulleit.

"Safety meeting," Jake shouts, as he takes a snort of cocaine. I despise Jake's sense of humor and somehow like him. "Let's get an idea of our talents before we blow up a car," he says.

"No pointing a gun at anything you don't plan on shooting. Always exchange guns pointed up and unloaded. Always call out 'down range' and 'cease fire' when crossing the firing line. You first, new guy."

My hands are still, my nerves cooperating, as I breathe deeply, hold the breath before firing and gently squeeze the trigger, this the same physical and spiritual place from which I shot free throws in high school, muscle remembered from the same time of life.

～

Those high school memories of evenings shooting in the desert outside Phoenix are some of the stillest I've got, the evening desert sounds of the bugs and the birds waking or hunting, a rising thrum, church organ-ic. It couldn't be true that we often, let alone always, went shooting after a rain but the desert's smell, in the transformation from the ten-foot tall constant hanging curtain of dust into plated mud, the curtain dropped to the floor and soaked, the air then cleaned and thinned, the mesquite and acacia all around now in wet scentedness catching up to their visual crowding of the landscape, that after-rain smell steeps all the images I've got. My drunk stepfather effusive in his praise of my talents, hugging me tight, slapping my shoulder, kissing my head, an explosion of physical affection, like the dam that held Father's Touch from me had broken in him too.

I remember once, I hadn't eaten since breakfast and it was getting dark. I thought there wouldn't be food until we got back to town. He abracadabra'd an Arby's bag out from behind his back, ceremoniously unwrapped one of the five-for-five silver balls, held the sandwich aloft, and split it between us, mocking, I think, a sacredness the moment did possess. He served me as I sat on the open tailgate of his truck as he drank out of his to-go vodka on ice. He passed it to me and I drank one sip, managing not to cough it down.

I had no real understanding of what drunk meant; I hadn't ever been drunk. And although his drinking often anticipated his throwing things, most of the time only near my mother, it also was part of these sacraments. He did many things precluded, Father, by your reading of the gospels or by any moral compass worth a damn. But also, your morality, based on the bad things you don't do rather than the good you enact seems to have paralyzed you, built up dams of every sort. His messiness was frightful, lurching and sometimes evil but his compassion reached out, free-flowing, too, his sacraments served at an open table.

I don't mean to break your heart, Father, when I say this abusive alcoholic taught me more about love than you have, but it is the case, and perhaps a broken heart for you, oh Stalwart One, would be a great blessing.

Damn, I hurt. I have spent so many years in "I'm fine," it is a shock, this layer-by-layer realization that I am not, never have been, will be picking up pieces the rest of my life as I preach my self-hate toward diminishment. I am sorry for the shock it must be to you that we are not fine, that you have been, the you living in my head has been, more of an adversary than I was willing to say or think.

That trip, I think it was the same one, Wayne drove me home, just him and me, my stepbrothers, mother, brother, not around for some reason this time. Stopped at a light, a man gave him the evil eye for the way his hand lay affectionately on my teenage neck. Time slowed to nothing in the tense moment I saw the man looking, then saw Wayne see him. Sometimes Wayne reacted to these moments violently. It was odd to know he would always win the fight, could, if he wished, destroy a man. He was Mr.

Western States in his style of karate, Mr. Arizona as a bodybuilder, trained as both a sharpshooter and a medic in the Army. And dressed like a cowboy. I don't know if you knew his martial accomplishments or just how he carried himself, how his muscles sagged, sagged even in their stiffness, off his frame, like sandbags stapled, a frame that would have been relatively narrow without years of willful and near constant intervention to *build* it into that edifice. Whatever you knew, you never saw him end an argument with a single punch, or—just to impress—a single high kick, when it had only just begun, conjuring that lightning even and especially when his last step had been a drunken stumble.

Running, complicit at ten or eleven or twelve, from some man or thing he had smashed and to his truck, peeling away, was a ritual of approximately annual frequency. Your occasional shouting matches with him were deeply unnerving for an already anxious kid, as I knew you didn't know, at least not with the concrete examples I'd been given, just how quickly and catastrophically things could derail for you with him.

Wayne looked back at the man giving the evil eye, peering through the thick air, until the man backed down by looking away. Wayne smiled at me and laughed, that victory enough for him this time. I sighed with relief and we drove on, his weights-calloused thumb rubbing my neck.

⁓

I empty the magazine of its seven rounds, hitting my marks four times. From thirty yards and about twenty years, I'm pleased with my performance.

"Nice," Jake says.

The drugs are flowing as the others take their turns. Jake is a quality shot, which isn't easy with the AK they all favor, which I know because I once snuck away to shoot with the more extreme gun folk of my day, the AK then the talisman of that extremism, as the AR is now, a secret I had to keep from both you and my stepfather. Things only begin to feel uncontainable in that languid, sloppy, drugged way it seems I'm now coming to know outside of movie viewing, when Ray empties an AK clip, failing to hit a vulture in flight a hundred yards away. I'm relieved. I was raised by a target shooting gun family, not a hunting gun family, and killing animals, especially in the larkish way Ray was trying to, repulses me. We never discussed competing philosophies on life-taking; no one, strictly speaking, has broken the minimal safety regulations Jake set forth. Reality, as I've understood it, is loosening but not unstuck—yes the rules about which substances can get used, and at what times of day, have been broken but nominal gun safety seems to be holding—as we move to shooting the music video, wherein we kill a car.

Jake fancies himself the director of this project. He places us all with care as he sets up multiple iphones on tripods and carries others in his hands. As we shoot the car, Jake hovers, cowers, follows and shoots some rounds himself.

He shows me some footage in slow motion as he plays his band. Set to surf-rock and slow motion, the machismo has gone comic. Maybe this video will be good.

"Down range," I shout, as I go to piss behind the only bushes around. I make eye contact with all and they nod in response, point their guns skyward. Having no holster or case, I've put the .45 in my jeans waist, this practical solution also an entirely unreasonable one, to the me of a couple hours ago, at least. But. It does feel good, warm and powerful against my hip, this casual familiarity with a death machine a feeling I haven't dared feel since I was just newly and merely technically a man. No, in recent years, I've been so mindful to distance myself from violence that I've been unwilling to touch its tools, implemented even on inanimate targets.

I have to walk directly down range until I make it about to the car, at which point I take a right toward a stand of creosote. As I'm standing there, I spot an old, beat up sleeping bag in the dirt, surrounded by plastic bags and flies. It's probably been there for weeks but it creeps me out. I pack up my genitals and waltz off.

As I come out of the brush and turn back toward the others, I'm about five yards to the side of the Impala. Ray shoulders his rifle, the others laughing as he does, and fires at the car to my right, shattering a window that sprays shards a foot from me. This move is apparently designed to fuck with me, as I remain down range, and fuck with me it does. I react, getting low, my hand instinctively travelling toward my hip, hovering over the pistol there.

Ray doesn't like this. He points his AK at me.

"Okay, Ray," Jake says.

Ray is silent as I slowly raise my hand and move it away from my hip to join my other hand in the air.

"Ray," Paulo says.

Ray smiles, unshoulders the rifle, laughs and, without sighting, pops a round off in my general direction, the intent seems to be, which hits me in my right shoulder.

II

"The fuck," I manage, before touching the wound, bleeding plenty, but just more than a graze, I realize, and fear veers out of its lane and into anger. I go at Ray, who in shock at his better aim while not aiming, is standing frozen. I grab the AK by the forestock with one hand, and pop his nose with a front punch with my other. This punch, also, I learned from my stepfather, repeated for bloody hours on the makiwara board. I wonder how much of him there will be in this day before it's done.

Ray falls to his knees. I stand over him, clearing the chambers and ejecting the magazines from both our guns, throwing them away from us.

"Okay, okay," Jake says, as he takes the guns from us with full consent.

"I'm sorry," Ray says.

"There's no such thing as a practical joke with live fire, you fuck," I tell him, as the rage drips back off me. I take my shirt off and wrap my shoulder.

"You okay," Jake asks me.

"Perfect aim, in a sense," I say.

"That was kind of bad ass," Paolo says to me, which I respond to by crying. No one knows what to do with this.

It all felt too good, the death tools, the rage, breaking another man's face in revenge and, most of all, having the cool kids finally acknowledge my rightful place. I can't stand to know how much I enjoy these things still. You reflexively scorn the phrase "toxic masculinity" as quickly and virulently as you do "black lives matter," Father. But what could be more toxic than this drive, and talent, for smashing people? What could better reveal the lethality of this drug than the come down? I wonder if you've just decided to stay fixed forever, push the come down off til after the rapture.

"Let's pack up," I say.

I chase down the magazines I tossed away, back over by the dead car. As I lean down to pick them up, I look back at the stand of creosote, where, on top of that beat up sleeping bag, a pair of eyes stare back at me. I approach, the man blinks. And then he's running. Running like hell, shouting in Spanish at the woman now at his side.

The guys over by the van see. I look at them to monitor their reactions for malicious intent, as shots have been fired at living beings including myself. The betas look to Jake for what to do. I stare Jake down, using whatever fresh alphaness I have to sway him if swaying is needed. He shrugs and turns away. I'm relieved.

"Illegals," Ray asks, on the way back to the car.

"Guess so," Jake says.

"No person is illegal," I say. And that ends it, somehow. Because I am now living in the afterglow of my assertion of might, I feel just fine reciting this liberal tenant, which I happen to believe, but the fact remains it's a trite thought I'd never simply parrot in another context. My might quiets, also, any objections from them. How gross, this power I've obtained.

And how directive. When we get back to The Loft, I find Janey in the kitchen, walk to her and kiss her. She kisses me back, putting her hand on the back of my neck, where the hairtips have stood up to reach back to her fingerstips. I say it's my fleeting testosterone surge that directed me but this is too self-deprecating. It's also the fear of death. I spent most of the drive home thinking how dangerous things were, how close for me and Ray and the fleeing migrants. In a world of AKs and car wrecks, I didn't want to fail to kiss her.

She looks at us all, sees our disarray.

"What happened," she asks.

"The new guy's good with us," Jake says. Janey laughs.

"I wasn't wondering what you thought of him."

～

It's evening. Janey and I walk through the fields beside The Loft. She holds my hand, an intimacy I've missed since long before I left Leah. Our sexual dysfunction had shown itself to be so much more than that, a dry place for emotional connection, spiritual communion, grade-school level boy-girl touch. I tried to believe it was only about sex because this was a crass need, I had learned, which I could just shame myself over and be finished with. But of course intimacy is unbounded, and shame never finishes with you. We never figured out how to balance our needs—her need to not have the desires of a man directing her behavior, as the men of the church had since she was a child, and I wanted that for her too, my need for connection and affirmation, which had, for nearly forever and always, been a hole in my life. This isn't entirely your fault, Father: my mother's bleeding needy heart, my stepfather's push-pull, didn't teach me health either.

I'd always thought my needs were shit, been taught by my church that marriage isn't there to make you happy, bub, but to make you more Christlike—who was crucified, you'll recall. So then suffering in marriage isn't merely acceptable, it means you're doing it right. Misery as affirmation.

The last few months of our marriage, in which I began to question what the church had told me about marriage and began to wonder if maybe my desires weren't shit—were perhaps only as dirty as piss or, dare I one day for one moment believe, not dirty at all—were a frightening time. I had swallowed so much shame for ever considering a marital reality other than my own. To a system so poisoned, the thought of moving away from the status quo, even if toward medicine, is a cataclysm, a cataclysm that can send you running back into the safety of the poison. And I don't mean, here, the thought of moving toward divorce. I mean asking to be held.

"How long will you be here," Janey asks me, as her thumb worries over my fresh knuckle scrapes, my old knuckle scars, as we walk toward the mountains, the setting sun behind us pinking the clouds above them. I do a poor job of keeping the grimace in my chest off my face.

"I'd better leave tomorrow," I say.

"You have somewhere to be," she asks, the hurt splintering into her voice box.

"No. I'm in a bad place now, emotionally, and being with you seems . . . very dangerous."

She has stopped our walk. She lifts my hand toward her chest, where there are raven's wings tattooed, fanning out all the way to her shoulders, I see. I see.

She touches my scars to her scars, my four knuckles nearly aligning with the four notched scars on her chest, above her heart, some teenage penance or letting of pain that's been reclaimed as the space between raven feathers. She opens my palm and puts it on her sternum. It's hard to say to my Puritan self, and to you, my Dear Purist, this isn't sexual. But it is not; it is even more threatening than the sexual.

Her heart is beating like hell.

"I won't hurt you," she says. "And I didn't ask you to look out for me."

"I'll hurt myself," I say.

She looks back at me with such a thrown look, questioning, I wonder, whether the man before her is now talking about suicide, which makes me certain I look even less stable than I feel. And so I clarify:

"You know what that kiss will cost me? In shame dollars?"

She shakes her head.

"I know what pity looks like. I don't even resent it," I say. "I am pitiful, and I fucking hate it. I'd love to be strong and convinced, like I was for twenty minutes out of my day—"

"Which included that kiss."

"Yeah," I say, shrugging. "You know what a night in your bed would cost?"

"Not that you've been invited."

"No, I'm sorry. I—"

She laughs, even in this enjoying putting me on the defensive of another front.

"But what would a night in my bed gain you?"

And I am crying. To be invited into someone's bed. What a sacred thing, I know I will always believe.

"I'll go tonight," I say. I'm shaking my head, knowing what she wants from me, what I want out of myself, just is not there. "I'll go just after this sunset."

She lets me stay. We sit in the dead tall grass, ants all over us, my head on her shoulder, as we listen to evening come online. I remember being walked out by you, at the age of ten, to the grassy mound on the edge of the golf course, this moment in time before the ruin of single parenthood for my mom, the ruin of divorce settlement and market downturn for you. You walked us out, me and my brother, James, you sat us down and explained to us about divorce in general and about this divorce, about our mother being a good woman, just the wrong woman. I'd had friends go through divorce by then, always with stories of spectacular fights. You yelled occasionally, histrionically displayed your white male privilege to anger as I did today in the desert but never had I seen a fight between the two of you, that I recognized as a fight. We sat there on that hill, overlooking the impossible green of a Paradise Valley Golf Course within a desert, as your explanations droned on. We used to picnic there on Sundays. I learned to ride my bike there. I don't think I heard a word you said after sentence three of your preamble. It was August, and so as humid as the desert gets. The sun had set behind horizon-wide cumulus clouds, the Palo Verde beetles were out. The golf course sprinklers swept back and forth in their impossibly long arcs as I spread my hands over the grass beneath me, gripped handfuls of the blades, careful, as I clenched them in my hands, to hold them just loosely enough to keep from tearing them out from their roots, then spread my hands out flat again and repeated. I have no idea what James experienced then, just as I have no idea what you said. I was in my own emotionally overdeveloped ten-year-old head in which, "Why here, why here, why here, why here," reverberated.

Janey and I sit, a view of the mountains to the east and west, the hills to the south. I realize these are all the visible landmarks of her home, the ones she sees when waking or returning or looking out her kitchen sink window, where I'm saying this goodbye. But that's both my shame and my self-flattery. This goodbye doesn't mean what yours did, this place is not her home like Sanna street was mine.

"Why do you care about me," I ask Janey. "You don't even know me, really." I believe my subculture has warped everything, all valuations, that a kiss and a hand-hold couldn't mean to her what it does to me.

"Would it be easier for you if I didn't care?"

"That's the first time you've sounded like a therapist to me."

I laugh, trying to make light, but she won't let me.

"I asked you a question," she says.

"I'd be very sad if you didn't care about me."

She puts her head on my knee.

"Good," she says.

17

Shame Baseball

DO YOU REMEMBER, FATHER, the day you chose a spring training game as the setting to publically shame me? Or was it mundane to your mind, not rising to the criteria of longterm storage? It was toward the beginning of the period I'm ending with these pages, after my mother's death, where I'd decided to stop having beliefs and opinions around you, as I didn't have the reserves of bullshit tolerance to contend with the onslaught of your correction.

Curious about my best friend Salt, who you'd met on a couple occasions including my wedding, you had looked up some of his performance art on the internet—there was public nudity involved—and its perversity had you wondering how my church could condone such a man, how I could minster to, befriend and live with such a man and, yes wait for it . . . *call myself a Christian.* You asked that question after remarking on the impressiveness of this here new White Sox spring training facility and lamenting the power of big market teams in baseball. You asked this question surrounded by dozens of strangers. Staring at that field as you launched into your indictment, I was sent back to Little League, hearing you shout your corrections at my unathletic self for not being like you (All State) or my brother (All State).

Then I was back to surveying my mother's picture shelf after her death, finding my little league photo pin, big and proud as a presidential campaign button. Four years old, a Pittsburgh Pirate squeezing that bat as tight as my chubby angel hands could.

I remember being at bat for the first time in teeball, you shouting *Choke Up! Choke up!* your face red raging. Unschooled in the language of baseball, I stretched my chin to the sky, cut off my breathing and clenched my throat in a shivering exertion. To my mind and experience, of course my father was commanding me to choke myself in public with the power of my mind.

$$\sim$$

I guess you'd been warming up to your spring training indictment of me, convicting and reconvicting yourself of the moral imperative to communicate your judgment each time your weak flesh wavered in the face of hurting your son.

It's been many years since I lived with you and I've realized something from what others have taught me of love: your working definition of it embraces its relational opposite—shame. You are so convinced you must hold stridently to the belief that individuals or whole groups are dirty, evil, or damned—that the loving thing to do is to call your child a failure—that when actual love comes up in your heart, I imagine you must shun it, convinced it is not love but weakness. How sad, to be starved of love and be so unable to recognize it that you cast it out. It is a stranger to you; you've made it one. This pattern in you primed me well for the *love the sinner, hate the sin* horse shit from the church. I was already accustomed to a demented version of love, which counts conditionality as a virtue.

I just sat there and took your barrage, managing no more than "I'm sorry to hear you feel that way." I felt the urge to run out of the stadium, Uber to the airport and be done with you, but of course I didn't. I've been so well conditioned to sponge your shame; I can't suddenly repel it when doused.

This was a surprising moment to me. For a few months you had flipped your typical triangulating, James had done something or I had or some mood had struck you and he was occupying the Least Favorite Son role then, as had only happened for a few stray weeks in our history. Later that day, away from the spell cast by your shame, I was texting James about how horrid, how unbelievable, how unfatherly your actions were.

"You're just very different people," he said. "You've both got to learn to just live and let live."

I could tell you'd also been texting him about our encounter and texted him as much. Then I used the actual phone function on my phone.

"No," is how I started the call. "I need you to tell me that shit was fucked. That I've done nothing to deserve that. And I need you, when he talks shit about me, to stand up for me, Big Brother. *That* is your role."

I was crying, as I always tried to avoid with either of you, trying to stay out of the *dismissed* box you each put Mom in when she got emotional.

"Okay," James said, and I exhaled for the first time in hours.

18

Her Sleeping Breath/Goodbye Ventura

AFTER THE SUNSET I sit there as still as I can, as Janey's sleeping breaths, rhythmed as to a metronome, breeze the hairs on my knee. I can feel her breath on me as I can feel God's breath in the air, tickling my left, westward facing, ear. I wait on that threshold, where the sun is down but Janey is still touching me, stealing half an hour's time, until daylight is burned all the way down. What a sacred time, to steal time, steal sleep with her, steal another moment in this heaven before God knows what purgatory is down whichever highway is the next.

In that flat darkness I wake Janey by stroking her hair, her hair which is totally unlike Leah's, from any woman I've been with, even and especially different from that one girl with white person dreads. The texture of Janey is as exciting as it is frightening, reminding me I'm in the wilderness from all I've known.

Janey blinks, bleary, at the surprising night. She looks to me, about to cry, I think, looking hurt that I'd let her sleep through our time, before connecting to whatever it is she sees in my face, which turns her expression also to gratitude. In silence she walks me to my car. She embraces me and that is goodbye.

I turn to my car. There is the gray upholstery of the back seat, which I for some reason notice now, which I can't notice without seeing flashes of my first girlfriend, making out with her in that backseat. Playing that strange evangelical game of slowly approaching and quickly retreating from maximum arousal, lest a climax be reached—the mess of the climax brings, I suppose, the proof of the sin and so must be avoided to maintain plausible deniability of the sin, with yourself, with your girlfriend, with your youth group interrogators. Playing that approach/retreat game continually and for over a decade longer than most, as I later found out no one else was even as serious as I was about this *purity* stuff. But there I was, a teenage evangelical Christian with tantric level orgasm control. It is laughably and embarrassingly silly to me here and now. It is this embarrassment that courses through me as I shake my head out of that memory, back into this moment leaving Janey. The embarrassment wraps me and I feel as silly about my time with Janey as my times in that backseat.

Neutral Milk Hotel comes on, blaring, as I turn the ignition. Wary of what it might play in her, I try to silence it before she can hear, which I know I don't—anyone with the album's own button can ID any of these songs three notes in. I drive down the long access road to the highway. I turn from south to north to south again.

As I drive, Pastor Steve calls me. It must be the thirtieth call I've gotten from church staff since I left and the first one I've answered.

"Hello, Steve," I say.

"You need to come back to Los Angeles and be with your w—"

"Our fathers are our models for God. We seek out pastors who are like our earthly fathers to help cram our Heavenly Father into our safe, and insufficient, categories. So many of us come from horridly abusive places that when we find a less abusive place, it gets graded on a curve and labeled healthy. That is my church experience, I realize. You are a shitty father figure," I say, ending the call and blocking his number.

III

19

Sunset Beer

I DIDN'T FLEE TOWN immediately the day I left my wife. I went to Sunset Beer, where I'd spent so many nights with her, with the subchurch. I sank down into an old leather chair, exhausted and numb, about to drink my beer when one of Redeemed's elders walked across the room toward me. We'd worked together on the church's foster care initiative, which felt so good so deep down and still does, church work effecting a tangible differ-ence for our city and its most marginalized rather than whatever vision casting or message orienting we normally spent our time on. I knew him to be a kind man with a warm smile and large family, by LA standards, twenty years my senior. I was thinking I might run into someone from the subchurch at Sunset but Ronald wasn't one of us. He is a wealthy westsider.

"John," he said, and I knew by his dim tone he'd come bearing his disapproval. I sank lower still, thinking this game of Christian Love or Christian Shame coin-flipping, which we encounter every first moment we disclose *sin* to a *brother*, didn't quite have the odds I'd thought. Heads, heads, heads every time.

"Ronald." I didn't get up. This unbalanced him for a moment but eventually he launched in anyway, shouting down at me to be heard over the bar noise.

"John, I believe you're in sin and need to repent."

I drank half my beer before speaking, a multiple sip affair that afforded me the opportunity to condescend to him with a "one moment please, Sir" finger in the air.

"I left my wife today," I said. He stooped down to hear.

"What?"

I stood up, putting him into a jerky backpeddle.

"If you're gonna denounce my sin, you should take its full measure. I left my wife today!"

"Well, I, uh, I'm quite sorry to hear about that, but it does makes sense that in a time where you've failed to hold to Scripture's teaching in one area—"

I laughed in his face.

"You don't even fuckin know me, Ron."

He turned red.

"I thought I did. And I take you at your word, when you're preaching."

"Didn't you leave your wife before you came to Redeemed, Ron?"

By this point everyone near us had cleared space.

"I . . . have a divorce in my past."

"Come on, bruh. You came from another church that believed the same shit about divorce as Redeemed. Yuh know, I think I've figured out the rule on this: if you get divorced at one church where divorce is forbidden, you can move to another that believes the same and still be accepted because the new one, like the old, believes they alone hold the orthodoxy and so your accountability begins only after you've found the new true faith. Yeah?"

His forehead wrinkled and his nostrils flared.

"That been your experience, Ron? You could get away with it one more time, at minimum!"

"I'm praying for you, I am," he said through gritted teeth. "Why'd you leave Leah?"

"Ask the fuckin rumor mill, Ron. Why'd you divorce your last wife?"

A barback who'd been collecting glasses came over to us.

"Hey, guys. You're gonna need to go outside for this if you can't calm down," he said.

"What you think, Ron," I said. "You wanna?"

"I'll be praying for you," he said.

"I covet your prayers, Brother."

"May you come to see your error. May you be spared hell," he said, on his way out of the room.

I laughed, gobsmacked.

"Yeah, Ron. God's super pre-occupied with sending those you disagree with to eternal torture!"

Father, you don't know Ronald but my surprise was total. In all my prior experience, he was a kind and loving man. We had conversations steeped in compassion. And somehow all that time, he was a few charged words away from damning me. I know how angry I sound in this conversation. And I was. I know it names me a fool, which I'm beyond denying.

20

Rules

WHAT RULES THERE USED to be. Don't let Janey's breath fall on you, certainly don't kiss her, stare in awe at her rising and falling chest, let her sleep beside you, oh God!

What will Janey become to me? Some short thread of life I wish I'd tugged at?

I suddenly feel sympathy for the certainty-lust embodied by the rule extremists, even more than I did when I was a master rule craftsman myself. I think of The Billy Graham Rule, followed by your vice president, which would've kept Janey even from my presence. Remember this rule—never meet alone with a woman other than your wife? Somehow, I long for that certainty, with Janey's warmth still lingering beneath my skin, a life I could only have received by leaving, well at least vacationing from, the rules. What desperate and damaged children, in need of such clear borders to yes and no, are they, am I. Perhaps forever.

My Dear Pavlov, I've been petrified in my life because of The Rules. You conditioned me to expect some perfect way of acting, which I must divine situation by situation in order for things to go well for me. Even once I decided, as a teen, that your rules weren't The Rules, I still needed to believe The Rules were out there to be found and followed and the evangelical church was more than happy to fill that space, telling me they were there in black and white, their interpretation plain.

I learned from you that every choice has a right or wrong and, in your mind, especially but not exclusively after your evangelical turn, this right or wrong was a good or evil.

In my memory, it's the most arbitrary rules that stand out. You despised mayonnaise, unable to even look at it, and wouldn't allow it in the house. Mom, starved of it, would put it on everything when we were at lunch without you. You once grounded James for saying the word in your presence. And I despise it too; it turns my stomach. I wonder with no way of knowing how I would feel about it if my mind were my own.

I can let go of whatever pleasures mayo may have offered me. But other things, too, turn my stomach because you taught me they should. *Effeminate* men, for example, and that does cost me—more to the point, it costs them—a great deal. And so I struggle against this ingrainment when it rears up. My high-minded philosophy overtakes my gut in time but my gut, endowed by you, gets the first word. What does its initial reaction look like, I wonder, to that already othered person, the *effeminate* man I meet on the street? What does my initial disgust, even if quickly replaced by a smile of willfully genuine compassion, do to his gut? I repent.

In my life I have been convinced, always, there is some other way to be that I'm missing. And so I just keep looking for it, keep interrogating myself as you interrogated me. I never find this perfect way, because that's not how the world is, any adult could see.

Your rules gained you my obedience as a child. Did you ever pause to ask, as you berated me, as you taught me to berate myself, what they would cost me as a man?

21

Cold Withholding, Need.

I WAS NEEDY IN my marriage to Leah and I am sorry to her for it. Your cold withholding, my mother's needy parentifying, the idealism I found in my faith, all had programmed me to pine for a wife who could satisfy my gaping physical and emotional needs. The church had told me marriage was a promised land of helpmate affirmations—no matter my professional failures and her justified financial fears—indelible spiritual connection—no matter the spiritual abuse she'd suffered—erotic, plentiful and on-demand sex—no matter sex's shame and abstinence-bred alienness to every part of ourselves. Leah's mother ("sex is dirty") and father (would not touch her) programmed her with a set of evangelical pathologies in perfect competition with my own. I was always too much for her, she was never enough for me, we blamed each other and ourselves. The resulting shame was vital. We could continue on in the church life we'd built, lopping off parts of ourselves, remanding them to various corners fenced off by shame, rather than losing that life. For quite a stretch at least.

22

Writing, Remembering

WRITING, TO ME, HAS been attending to the spiritual, jotting the sacred down before it evaporates, practicing remembering, the way those wise church parents ask their children to give thanks for something in their day at the dinner table. I am so surprised that writing this, sorrowful and angry as it is, feels the same as writing sermons, as journaling Spiritual Thoughts. Perhaps the distinction was never there, it was all sacred all the time.

23

Castaic

I END UP IN Castaic, about fifty miles east, in the somewhat shitty hotel bar across the road from my flatly depressing motel, just me and the bartender. There's a game on and the Dodgers are winning. I've been enjoying their good year. The energy it gives the neighborhood, on Sunset Boulevard near the ballpark, at The Shortstop and Sunset Beer and Masa, is electrifying. It's been a hot summer and unusually humid and all the neighborhood, out in that steam together, when the team is winning, is deeply connecting. It makes LA—my part of it at least—a walkable town where baseball is worn and talked, not just the city of people trapped in cars I imagine you imagine.

"I like Turner," the bartender says, gamely.

"I do too," I respond too quickly, starved of conversation. "I live a few blocks from the stadium. Used to. He's the only player I ever thought looked like a dude from the neighborhood." I realize that I mean a white dude from the neighborhood, and despite my guilt, don't apologize.

"What you do for work," the bartender asks. I'm three beers in, and so . . .

"I'm a writer."

"Movies and TV?"

"Pseudo-religious nonfiction," I say, smirking mostly to myself.

"Cool," he says, without asking for elaboration. He turns from me, starts fiddling inside a drawer next to the cash register. He returns with an index card.

"What you think of this," he asks, handing me the card.

Most of us understandably start the journey assuming that God is "up there," and our job is to transcend this world to find "him." We spend so much time trying to get "up there," we miss that God's big leap in Jesus was to come "down here." So much of our worship and religious effort is the spiritual equivalent of trying to go up what has become the down escalator. I suspect that the "up there" mentality is the way most people's spiritual search has to start. But once the real inner journey begins—once you come to know that in Christ, God is forever overcoming the gap between human and divine—the Christian path becomes less about climbing and per-formance, and more about descending, letting go, and unlearning. Knowing and loving Jesus is largely about becoming fully human, wounds and all, instead of ascending spiritually or thinking we can remain unwounded. (The ego does not like this fundamental switch at all, so we keep returning to some kind of performance principle, trying to climb out of this messy incarnation instead of learning from it.)

I read it three times over, experiencing some paranoia over the philo-sophical attunement I'm getting from a bartender in Castaic.

"You wrote this," I ask.

"It's Richard Rohr."

"I don't know who that is," I say.

"He's a friar. In New Mexico. Went to one of his retreats once. What do you think?"

"It is very good," I say.

24

Toast Memory

Mom would always burn the toast. She was this masterful cook, but the French bread pizza or the cheesy toast or the damn rye bread for bacon and eggs never made it out alive. I was a chunky kid, you'll remember, especially when I turned to food for comfort after the divorce, and Mom showed care for me by fattening me up. I remember one night dinner was late, as always, but still delicious, Mom, James and I sitting around the table smiling nervously at one another, unsure of what the new post-divorce routine ought to look like. This was in the small house she rented off Cactus, before Wayne entered the picture. I would have been just less than eleven at the time. She was shaky in those months, a particularly guilty mother, a particularly guilty alcoholic.

She jumped up from the table and pulled open the smoking oven to the black garlic bread inside. I imagine her wine glass sloshing in her hand as she rushed about but that's not an honest part of this memory. She pulled the bread out, burning her hand through too thin a kitchen towel, slapped it down on the counter and fell into a ball on the floor, crying. James looked across the table with your own disgust. He takes after you, not only in looks but in temperament, just as I took after Mom. *Took.* She's been gone long enough to push my characterological assignations into the past tense.

I went over to her, sat next to her, but she wouldn't embrace me. I picked up the garlic bread and ate it, furiously trying to fix her, show her all was well, all was well, I was happy, mouth full of ash. She saw it as a show, herself as hopeless, and rejected the gesture. I honestly sort of liked that garlic bread. I was chubby: it was still salty carbs.

When Leah would come home from work, exhausted, angry and sad, taking it out on me, I would start furiously speaking her *love languages*, scrubbing dishes, vacuuming, apologizing for the actions of other people. I did this especially in our final weeks together, when she was working more hours to compensate for my quitting the church, hours she wouldn't have had to suffer if I'd kept my end of the bargain. I got mad about the unfairness of my one-sided and unrequited attempts to reconcile but couldn't find the means to stop my frantic fixing behaviors, which made me, I think, quite unattractive, just pushed her away further. To be honest about my desires, I wish with all I have I were there now, washing the damn windows, easing her homecoming, a homecoming that cannot come, a reality I'm kicking and screaming against.

25

Yucca

I PROCEED TO GET shit-canned with the bartender, which for me is five beers. He and I close the place at eleven and go out into the desert together. He has something to show me, he says. It's not that I don't occasionally think strangers are considering murdering me, it's that this stranger has proved his kindness.

Out in the desert, he pulls out a pocketknife and cuts open a yucca, giving me a piece of its insides.

"Eat it," he says.

He passes me his flask to wash down the nutty raw potato.

We lay down on the hood of his car, a level of comfort with male closeness I haven't had since high school at least, and look at the stars. The vast sprawl of LA has the night sky less than clear but this moment, where I bother to rest, bother to look up, has the stars blinking wearily back at me. What is a religious experience? Is it the same now as it ever was for me, just that life has me too tired to acknowledge the mystical? Or has my grizzling experience allowed me to rightly feel the bullshit in it now, that beauty was never Beauty.

But yes, it is beautiful. And I am religious at heart, I can feel. Or spiritual or whatever the fuck. I just don't want to deal with the baggage for a minute, want to tip a bellman to handle it all for just the one night at the fancy hotel I know I can't afford and am sure I don't deserve.

"What are you doing tomorrow," The bartender asks.

I nearly jump at the breaking of my teenage night sky reverie.

"Driving east."

"What's east," he asks.

"You said this friar's in New Mexico."

"Yes," the bartender says. "You should go to see him."

"I will," I say. I send the words out my mouth as a lie, as I hear them they convince me.

26

Children's Program

I VOLUNTEERED FOR THE children's ministry once, years ago. According to the calendar, it was time to read The Prodigal Son from the Storybook Bible. At this time, I was still considered a stable and pastorly presence in my church. The children came unto me, sitting in and around my lap.

Three pages in, I burst into tears, sputtering, my projectile crying hitting a child. Aghast Presbyterians ran to rescue the children from my emergent emotions.

There's no father on this earth like the Prodigal's father. To be fair, I don't think I'm humble enough a son to turn back to you, Father, like the Prodigal. How beautiful to think God can be such a replacement to us. But how could my categories, forged by you, Father, ever truly hold such a God? No, I've squeezed my concept of God, always, back into what you left me. The way The Prodigal story strains this container is excruciating, which pain is alarming to literal children as well as myself.

27

The Lesser Parts of Me

THERE'S A DISTINCTION I should make. I've said I don't want to hate you and I believe that's true, at least for the best parts of me and in my wisest moments. But I do need be angry with you. Culturally, we conflate the two, treating them both as toxic, which in their expressions they often are. But this is an error. Anger, I think, can serve us well. I think it served Christ. Perhaps I'm assuming too much of my capacity for righteousness in anger. Perhaps any anger I could ever feel is toxic, made so by my own searing imperfections of character, of which I am constantly aware. But I think burying my anger, under forgiveness in name only, under distancing, under *I'm fine*, has guaranteed an eruption.

28

Counselor

I'm driving east on the 10, as I've done so many times to visit you, Father, or my mom for whatever fraught holiday. I used to pride myself on getting the trip done in the middle of the night, no stops for gas, a five-hour stretch unimpeded by traffic, speeding strategically (how careful was my rule breaking).

Today, I'm cruising and side-tracking. I'm near the main entrance to Joshua Tree and I'll be curving the 60 miles through the park to its back side, back down to the 10. There is a café here I visit every time I come. Big meals before or after a long hike. I've always come alone to get away from LA to pray or write and it's strange now to feel a familiar place that isn't stained with the loneliness of Leah memories. Strange to feel happy in the present and past of a place as my lone self.

I am eating at the breakfast bar, which in this small town becomes an actual bar in the evening hours. A woman about my age sits down next to me. I'll call her Allie.

"Hi," she says, giving her name.

"I'm John," I say and shake her outstretched hand.

We make casual conversation about the day and the food. I can see her getting fidgety as I edge toward finishing my meal.

"What do you do," she says, after I ask for my check. It's a normal question but she blurts it into desperate abnormality.

"I'm in between jobs," I say.

"What was your last job," she asks, searching, as I dread some part of me still is pastorly, that I've been found out.

"I was a pastor," I sigh.

"A pastor of a Christian church," she asks, confirming her treasure hunt.

"I think Christians are the only people who'd use that word."

"I was at Morongo Valley Baptist for twenty years, just until recently." I remember church-naming as credential offering from my evangelical days, *Bible* or *Baptist* dropped in the title to let you know they subscribed to all the best rules. But I have compassion for it. She wants to know she's known. "That's where I live. Did you counsel people?"

"What's on your mind," I ask.

"I need someone to talk to about a problem," she says.

"I really am not qualified to do that." I've been looking away for a couple sentences. Finally looking back, I see how shattered she is.

We walk. Up and down that main road, Twentynine Palms Highway. Allie tells me her husband's been beating her for three years and she's beginning to think she'll leave. Allie is far from the first woman to tell me she's being abused by her husband.

I don't know what in me could attract this confiding. I am a man brought up by men, you and my stepfather, around other young men, my brother and stepbrothers, taught by still other men, professors and pastors, for whom masculinity was the language and the air. My mother was a great influence on me but she breathed that air too, spoke the father-tongue well.

Although the confiding began with men telling me about their abusive childhoods, a year in, women began coming. Maybe the women had to wait until I'd been made safe, could sense that I'd developed the ability to hear these horrors with the training wheels of man-to-man compassion. Given gender dynamics in the church, that must not have been easy for them. Given the church's theology, their only choice of pastor was me or another man. Graded on a curve, apparently, I'm sa*fer*. In my short time spent counseling at Redeemed more than ten women told me they'd been beaten or raped. The first time it happened, I nearly lost my mind. Gabby, I'll call her, a member of the westside church, came to me during my limited office hours and detailed years of physical abuse by her husband. He *disciplined* her with a belt, if she stayed out late or failed to return his texts. If she were, upon returning home, then insubordinate, he would punch her in the stomach and body, never the face. Gabby wore a lot of sweaters. I have, since that moment, always wondered if all women who wear sweaters in the summer are covering—damn the pun—for abusive men. Not very many women do it and there are many abusive men: does that math work out precisely, such that any summer sweater spotting should automatically trigger a husband punching?

Her husband didn't attend church with her and their children, was not a member of our community; he did use exclusively Christian rationalizations for his behavior. Our church didn't support staying in abusive marriages—as many evangelical and *Reformed* churches do—but the fact is that Gabby felt uncomfortable seeking a divorce as a member and uncomfortable talking about it with anyone else on the pastoral staff, ever. That should have told me something louder and sooner about the implicit messages church, even a church like ours, sends on systems of abuse.

"I should forgive him, shouldn't I," Gabby asked me.

I told her about Desmond Tutu's understanding of unforgiveness— drinking poison and expecting it to kill your enemy. So forgiveness is what we gift ourselves so we can move forward in freedom, having unburdened ourselves of the luggage of what others have done to us. But we Christians often conflate reconciliation with forgiveness, when that is a further step that isn't guaranteed, is often destructive and unsafe. Forgiveness need not mean the continuing of a relationship. And forgiveness probably takes time and distance. I think maybe I had it wrong: I'm not sure it was Tutu who said that, any of it.

Then I told Gabby "I think you should get a divorce," that years-long abusers don't suddenly stop, in my experience, no matter the prayers, no matter the faith, that God cared for her and her need for healthy relationships. I cried angry tears with her, which meant something to her, I think, but which I see now as quite selfish, a privileging of space for my male anger at a hurt not my own, over and against her feminine sadness for a hurt that lived in her body. In her children's bodies.

I can imagine how wrongheaded my therapist friends would find my counsel. But given the yawning gap between good therapy and *Christian Counseling*, at least I didn't throw a handful of bible verses at her. At best, this dismisses the realness and particularity of a hurt, at worst it would have dipped Gabby in shame. It's the softserve ice cream, shelled in chocolate, I have in mind when I think of this dipping; I see former pastors, or you, Father, leaning out the slide window of the box truck, asking "Sprinkles on that?"

I know my therapist friends never tell anyone what to do; they don't think it helps. But I also felt she needed to know that I, A Pastor, was forcefully recommending what she felt was forbidden. I was trying to license her. This permission slip wasn't mine to give, of course. Only because other males had disenfranchised her was I in a position to counsel her—but there I sat, in that position, thinking to try and use it for good. I wonder if there's any therapist who would license my choice.

And then I followed her home. Nursing my revenge fantasies against her husband for the thirty-minute drive, never thinking of turning the car around, never thinking maybe—as I did every day for weeks afterward—this is fucking crazy, and selfish like my tears. I parked across the street from her house and watched. They lived on a busy street. Mine was one of five cars parked across from their house and not the closest but when she looked in my direction as she walked from the carport to her front door, she caught me dead in the eye. She was glad to see my familiar face for a tiny moment, that little happy accident when two LA lives intersect outside their usual LA roads and the brain autoregisters joy, before a grim fear seized all the real estate on her face. She froze there, on the granite of her desert landscape yard, halfway between her car and the front door.

"I understand," her sad nod said, her eyes so clear and connected, none of the ashamed looking away of our counseling session left on her. "But please don't," her headshake said. "Your help is no help," said her eyes, as she walked on.

I nodded, turned the ignition and pulled away. As I U-turned past their house, I saw her husband greet her at the door with a hug that looked genuine and loving; it occurred to me that perhaps he is a little boy acting out of the hurt he was brought up in, that perhaps seeing him as a Child of God could activate my compassion for him, had he been the one to seek me out. But that interpretation was instantly unavailable to me the moment I pulled away. I've nursed my hate for him ever since, kept myself from the husband punching reflex which has grown in me, in many many church services since. I am not proud of that. I believe Christ would have me show radical compassion for those who've committed even the most grievous sins. And I believe solving a woman's sadness, solving a woman's life, with my anger, is a grave sin of its own.

But that doesn't stop me from feeling in my bones that my fists can solve problems. Wayne taught me as much; they have in the past. I remember a bully from the fifth grade. The fucker had harassed a developmentally disabled kid for weeks. After pushing the disabled kid down, he was towering over him, surrounded by bystanding kids in a circle on the playing field. I came up behind him and turned him around by the shoulder. He immediately whipped his backpack at my face—a real cheapshot. My nose bled profusely and my shirt was quickly soaked. He backed up, a dumbfuck smile on his face, which immediately disappeared when I kept coming, bleeding, at him. He swung again and I was ready. I caught the bag, ripped it away from him and threw it on the ground as I stomped at him. He slapped and punched while I deflected the best I could until he fell on the ground and I got to tower over him, menace his dumb ass. Never threw a punch. So maybe it isn't my fists that solved anything. Just my toxic masculinity in a noxious dose. He never hit another kid as long as I knew him. I felt so badass when I wouldn't tell any teacher, any parent, where my bloody shirt and nose came from.

I can think of him compassionately now, feel guilt even, for the shame that happening must have put on him.

But also fuck that guy. Fuck all ya'll abusers.

29

A Simple Question, Really

"WHAT DOES GOD WANT," Allie asks me, drowned out as a semi-truck slams past us on the Twentynine Palms Highway. I can only tell what she said because I've been asked this so many times I've memorized the lip movements.

"I don't know," I say.

"What should I do?"

"I don't know."

Allie's breathing is heavy and anxious.

"What did you used to tell people like me?"

"All the wrong things." The sun is stark, the shadows cast by it vibrating their defined forms on the hot pavement, all so in-focus it's assaultive. I don't think I'd hear a pin drop on the ground but I'm certain I'd feel its vibrations on my chest through my shirt. "I'm sorry I'm the ex-pastor you sat next to," I tell her.

She nods.

"I lived with my great aunt while my mom was in rehab. My brother sexually assaulted me. I was *nine*," she says, *nine* ringing like a warrior call from some aggrieved protestor standing before a tank, stronger yet for the certainty she will get no justice. She's already been flattened. And the flattening continues. "My great aunt knew, I know she knew, she didn't care. Well, she did care. She told me it was my fault."

"I'm sorry," I say. I am holding her hand in both of mine, no lovers' perpendicularity but all three of our hands parallel to the ground like a sandwich, like a catholic priest would hold a hand, I imagine. The skin on the back of her hands is old-woman papery and so soft to my touch.

"My mother's brother raped her. She told me when she got out of rehab and picked me up. Her mom locked her in the basement for an hour when she found out. Set an egg timer."

She nods. And nods. And nods, looking to the mountains out to the east, the north, the south. Our hands are shaking. I don't know who started it but it is now locomotive.

"I got family in Utah," she says. "Thank you," she says, and hugs me. I watch Allie stride to her truck and drive East. This is the direction of Utah and not of the Marengo Valley.

30

Holding

DEAR GOD WHAT GOOD could *I don't know* do the souls we minister to. But think of what it would cost us. Our identity as Answer Holder. Our business model is being sure. And that is bitterly funny to me.

A faith that holds to an infinite God and a finite human mind must be fundamentally agnostic. That's not an original thought. I first read it, as an eager evangelical teen, in a theology text by an old white man, a guardian of the orthodoxy. It was a book of *systematic theology*. Yes, a man who acknowledged the unknowableness of God didn't shrink from systematizing Him. We are deaf to irony.

31

Swing Low

I STOP ALONG THE drive to hike. At the top of a rock pile mountain, reclined and looking out over the short shadows, down at a valley full of hundreds of Joshua trees, their popcorn blooms, less than annual, fat like Christmas tree toppers, I'm shaking with lucky joy, transported beyond myself, overwhelmed by the goodness always at hand if one stops to look. This before plummeting into a blanketing despair, where the desert is no garden but a wasteland indeed, a despair that covers all my past life, loves and actions, paints my future in the certainty of a lonely death.

On this train, for many years, suicide was the inevitable and gnawing terminus of my ruminations. "The thought of suicide is a great consolation; by means of it one gets through many a dark night." Pastor Steve quoted that bullshit of Nietzsche's at me one Sunday years ago when I shared my testimony of mental health struggles in front of the congregation. This sentiment is as grave and ignorant as that "permanent solution to a temporary problem" bit one hears from church talkers of your generation.

I guess Steve thought this would be some dark bro-down, some wink letting me know he was part of some terrible in-crowd. Suicide came to me cognitively, as an escape plan, but offered no cognitive comfort, as Nietzsche claimed to have found. It always seemed, no matter how heavenly minded I may have been at a given moment, to be a plan for which window of a burning skyscraper to jump out of—trading immolation for an abyss. But the pull toward suicide didn't just come cognitively and in despair. It also came reflexively, often, an itch jumping up to the skin begging to be scratched, an impulse I feared I'd lose the power to deny, be caught by undefended.

I shouldn't have shared my mental health issues with the church. It made my life harder, as I'm sure sharing with you will. I guess I'd hoped to spur some change in the way we dealt with these things as a community. I hoped a church like ours could be called to a greater depth of thought and compassion. It only served to alienate me further.

I've resisted the temptation to edit out what descriptors you could use to pathologize me, Father. I know it's served you to consider me unwell, ever since the damn school district psychologist's diagnosis of bipolar II in high school, which I always heard as "bipolar too," as though he knew, everyone knew, you certainly knew, of my inheritance from Mom. You've seemed nearly giddy over this diagnosis at times. Sensing the convenience of your labels, the way you've only ever asked me about my emotional experience—my tears or shouts or *pressured speech*—when we've been in disagreement, I've never given you the satisfaction of telling you about my particular roller coaster ride.

But the truth is that the contours of my ups and downs are inseparable from who I am, and that you must, one day, know me is the foundation for all this. I tried medication once and for six months experienced a narrower band of oscillation between high and low. I think it meant a lot to Leah, my new bride, that I would try for her. I cried fewer tears and less often. I experienced more muted reveries, which did make me wonder, even as a pastor in good standing at the time, how much of religion, my own and the prophets', is pathology. But however much religion I've got left, I believe this was wrongheaded, a questioning of my experience only available to me if I thought of my self as a thing to be cured.

I don't think my ups and downs are or have ever been what's wrong with me. I'm not easy for those who love me to handle, this isn't easy for me to handle myself. But it's not insurmountable, and it isn't my responsibility to be easy for you—I hope I can finally believe. I want to experience joy in my life as transporting and, damn it, the darkness in this world is devastating. I'm not wrong to be devastated by it. If my ups and downs were insurmountable, if they ever become that for me, I will feel a responsibility to myself and others to do what I must to survive. Maybe that's what the medication was for me, a crisis measure.

And so I can sit on this rock, feel joy and desperation in succession, without the fear that I'll try to fly or throw myself down. I can sit in this. I have dropped the expectation of those I love needing to sit with me. There may be much sadness and anger in what I'm writing to you and I know telling you this won't keep you from labeling and pathologizing me but I'm getting better, more able to talk to myself in it and know, in the moment, that moments don't last forever. I haven't had a proper delusion of grandeur or serious suicidal thought in many years now. When I think of my death now, it isn't something I want, isn't an action I fear I'll take, it's just, after leaving Leah, something I think I deserve. Not that you're entitled to know.

32

Strange Exercise,
Which the Sleep Psychologist Taught Me

As I try to sleep in my car at this campground, I'm caught ruminating on you. I focus on my breathing and perform the strange little exercise of raising and lowering my index finger along with my breath. But you keep my mind from mindfulness. You are the image that won't be held loosely, won't be let go down the river. You don't flow, Father.

I see you goodbying me. Your stiff eyes turned toward me at that golf course as you explained yourself, turned away from me at the White Sox spring training facility, turned away from me, myopically focused on the page by the rage of finality, reading this, oh Resolute One.

Forgive me, Father, I've mostly tried to keep the overtly political out of this, but in this time where so much of what separates us is manifested in the political, when you're goodbying of me is mirrored by your abandonment of every possible social obligation—my clearest articulation of current conservative thought—I don't know how. And the idea that the political can be segregated—from our discourse, from religious thought—seems a fantasy invented by, only attempted by, and to the exclusive advantage of middle class white folks.

I can't keep the political out of this because the personal, social, political gas-lighting we Christian youths received from you, our elders, was only made possible by the theological gas-lighting you first perpetrated. If we've been taught from the cradle to scoff at any who might point out Jonah's inability to live three days in the belly of a fish, why wouldn't we question science more broadly, when, for instance, scientists speak of climate change? If God's boundless love for life is boiled down to *pro-life*, which only means anti-abortion, why wouldn't we be co-optable into gun-love, and then even war-mongering? We youths were so well conditioned to be manipulated, not just by you patriarchs but by all possible future authorities. And you were self-conditioned, in turn, for this co-opting—don't think the oil men profiting from your votes doubt the fact of climate change; your religious fervor did give them quite the opening, though.

And so.

Some eon of weeks ago, your president, who you support unconditionally, it seems, gave that joint press conference with Vladimir Putin in Helsinki, where he took the side of that KGB officer over every American intelligence agency in particular and American interests in general. It hasn't left my mind, although it's been daily replaced by an ever-fresh controversy.

My God, what have you and yours been talking about when you say patriotism? It isn't that I think patriotism is an ultimate good but—I'm trying to understand you on your own terms—you always did.

You'll recall your indictments of Obama's *apologies* to our adversaries, the way you threw around the word *treason* during that time. Damned if your president's betrayal doesn't feel familiar, his transactional and triangulating affections. Our narcissist church fathers groomed us for his particular abuse, such that many of us ran into his familiar arms with their votes.

It's not that this is nearly his worst crime, or the one I care most about. Family separation at the border may be remembered as the darkest domestic policy of my lifetime; his implicit embrace of white supremacists in Charlottesville was a worse moral abdication and misuse of the bully pulpit than Helsinki. But I don't expect racial inequality to offend you. You had taught me to expect, however, that supplication to our adversaries would outrage you. I just wasn't prepared to believe white supremacy is in fact the core value in play, marionetting behind it all, even Patriotism, all along. I wasn't capable of that level of mistrust. The McCains and Doles of your party had so eloquently convinced me white supremacy was more a lamentable bug than a policy feature. But I simply don't know now how else you excuse your man's violations of your sacred patriotism than *at least the fellow doing it is white*.

I don't know what it is about Vietnam or the frightful hippies' free love or the *race riots* or that terrible spate of assassinations that so bent your generation but I would like you to please just stop. Stop inflicting your fatherly tough love on us, we're adults now.

We'd presumed your privilege would satisfy you, that your counting out the clock on what was left of the good old days, which we never got to see, would be good enough. That we could kindly ignore you while you lived out your days in plenty. But apparently the knowledge that left to our own devices, we would elect representatives black and female, that our electorate would get browner, motivated you to wade, with gumption, back into the *culture wars*.

We thought your greed could be sated by plenty, which faulty logic now makes me wince; that's not how greed works. No amount of more, of tax cuts, of shaming the poor with welfare-to-work that doesn't actually even provide, no accumulation of wealth and power, no decimation of the earth you won't be around to suffer, no degree of *purity* foisted upon my generation—purity to your narrow interests, where the political is theologized—is enough, it is finally clear. No price, including the abducting of *alien* brown children (party of family values) and the above aid and comfort to our adversaries (America first), is too high.

You who inherited the middle class and are so hell-bent on minority rule as to sell us to the Russians rather than the democrats, sell out democracy for autocracy, have the balls to tell my generation, whose college degrees got us jobs making lattes, that we act entitled. That is quite something.

We will be recovering from your greed, if we survive it, for generations after you're gone. I'm sorry we made the mistake of humoring you this long. But, so we can begin to recover, would you please just stop. Breathing, I mean.

33

Spilling

READING OVER WHAT I'VE written, seeing the ruthlessnes and glibness, I realize my sadness has gone to anger and my anger has pointed straight at you. Blame is a flamethrower. My weapon imprecise, I'm more imprecise yet: inebriated of my rage.

It's all bubbled over, spilling out over everything, staining whatever points of value or moral authority I might have had. I've said too much, censored too little, for this to be recognizable as a reconciliation project. My instinct is to go back and cover over some of it but I'm not going to. I can't withhold anymore. I pray—I still do, yes—that at the end of this we will both want to reconcile. But unless you know something more like all of me, it would be a hollow reconciliation, after which I'd just begin again to be held to a me that doesn't exist.

I'm scared to think of what this real reconciliation would take. I can think of twice you've apologized to me in a genuine way, repented let's call it. I believe you and yours have sinned grievously, that even if I am willing to forgive—I am, I believe—the repentance that reconciliation is predicated upon is just galaxies out of reach. The impossibility of your admitting even a minor fault, let alone an accounting for the enormity of your sin, makes the steps of reconciliation—reparations, let us say—laughably out of reach. I do laugh thinking of it. It's a bitter laugh but it's what comes up in me. God forgive me for my lack of hope.

34

Her Latest Descent

A COUPLE MONTHS AFTER Julia's death came my mother's. What a beautiful human she was and what faith, I fondly think now. Then I judged her for her lack of *orthodoxy*, told her to solve her loneliness by going to church, a *bible-believing* one, I said more than once, God forgive me. She held to God's love fiercely through it all, being divorced by you for being hard to deal with, having that divorce blamed on her by the church, where you were an elder and she was a Sunday school teacher. The divorce happened when she was forty; I was ten.

She had been doing better, drinking less, finally, God, at least when I saw her three months before her death. She came to LA for The Fourth of July and her birthday. James and his family came too, the one time they located a family trip in my town. They typically asked me, the one unencumbered by children, to be the one to fly to wherever it was they were for vacation and I, guilty over my lack of children, always had.

I remember Mom playing with her grandkids at the Splash Pad, careful to stay shallow and slow because she'd gotten dressed up fancy for brunch. My nephew Gus, just two at the time, had taken off his diaper and was putting his butt on a water jet because it felt good. I began searching for something to cover him and by the time I'd grabbed a beach towel and turned back to him, I saw mom in the fountain with him, covering him by hugging him and dancing with him, making a shame-free game of it for him, her Sunday best soaked through. She was laughing and locked on his face, the new joy of her embrace quickly overshadowing the loss of his butt shaking, which he held precious, as you know.

III

I don't know what switch flipped between this July joy and October, and then flipped into overdrive the last couple weeks she went whole hog, drinking all day, welcoming back in my ex-stepfather (she had finally left him a few years earlier). Wayne woke up to an insulated 32 oz. Thirst Buster™ mug full of vodka on ice every morning I lived with him and it seems clear his drinking never slowed in the intervening years. In my mind, he is a vampyric alcoholic, only able to hurt her because he was invited back in. She woke one of those sordid mornings—I saw the house after; it looked like two middle class 60 year-olds had been playing at Sid and Nancy for two weeks—bleeding from her esophagus. She refused medical treatment for hours. I was in Los Angeles. No one with the moral authority to insist was with her in Phoenix. When she finally asked to be taken in, the doctor expected recovery; there was no rush for my flight home, he told me on the phone. But her body was too diminished by alcohol to support her; everything failed in cascade. Two hours after his first call, the doctor told me to get a flight immediately and take a car directly to the hospital in Scottsdale.

I hadn't heard from her during this latest descent. I wasn't alarmed. Such drops in communication for a few weeks were common with her.

Just four years before, the same thing happened to her, coughing up blood in a Pittsburgh bathroom. She refused a trip to the hospital then too. I showed up then because of my grandmother's funeral, the same reason my mom was in town. I insisted she go to the hospital and drove her myself. She and the doctors told me—doctors and the things they think will comfort—they were sure she would have died had I not been there.

I ask you, Father, with this set of facts, who is so strong as to not blame himself for his mother's death? That man, is his well-adjustedness of such magnitude it bends reality, curving, not his conceptions toward the truth, but the universe to his will?

Give me guilt.

The guilt. The guilt won't stop whispering at *you could have saved her* or *her death is your fault. You killed her*, it says. This murder-guilt isn't some final destination in my emotional journey. It has become, since it was first prospected in the searching early days after her death, my starting place. Where there is pain, the guilt must explain it with *fault*, and I am a Calvinist somewhere still in my bones, so the fault is always always finally mine. And the fault must be extreme, so *murder*.

It's laughable to write this. I know I'd be alarmed to hear it from anyone I care for, rush to comfort them, argue them out of it. But God, I'm a liar if I don't transcribe the mumbling story in my head: *John, you killed her.* I'm more endangered if I avoid articulating it, leave it a mumble. The statement I can wrestle with. The mumble is quiet death. It is a mystery cancer, painless while it grew, excruciating now that it's taken over, diagnosed weeks before it kills me, I have in mind for this death.

I've wondered about that other option apparently available to people of our faith—the willful reality-bending—very much. I've seen you and many of my elders in the church struggle against the world that's plainly there, insisting upon another, which either you fear is lurking (The Gay Agenda) or hope you can hope into reality (recovery from stage 4 cancer). Your *hope* is manipulation, gaslighting us into thinking our pain is our fault. Your fear is malignant, driving you further from the world, spreading division even among those few who, for now, remain in your in-group.

I remember ten years ago, when you showed me your will to believe bullshit into being. My brother's wife had told me your wife had mentioned, multiple times, you were considering disowning me. I knew your wife's propensity for trying to reshape reality in this way, so I imagined her statements were a reflection of her wants, not your plans. It tore me up though, thinking about the possibility you'd give in. It surprised me how deeply I still cared, apparently, about your opinion of me. Awake in my bed nights on end, I felt shame over the shame I could still take on from you.

I confronted you on the phone. There was an oversized ad for Coke full of beautiful teens with surfboards, hanging on the façade of the Regal movie theatre along the 110 freeway downtown. I was looking at those laughing teens, stuck in traffic, when you denied both that you'd ever considered disowning me and the possibility your wife could have said it. My brother's wife was a liar, you said. That Coke ad was up for years. I think the rent was too expensive to fetch another tenant, the removal too expensive to bother getting it down. Whenever I saw that curly brown haired man, his wet suit half-hanging from his waist, laughing skyward in the throws of Coke-fueled joy, I revisited that flat statement from you: "That didn't happen. She's a liar."

Your sureness is so easy. Even though—because—it's a sureness over the most tenuous beliefs. If something is too hard to confront, it must be rejected, even if it's the state of things, the very condition of the world around you a negotiable. I have never been capable of this sureness, have sometimes wanted it. I suppose I'd always sensed the price was too high for me, even if I didn't quite understand the currency of the transaction. Today, on the other side of our old shared theology, I'd call that currency my self.

35

Codifying Poems

I NEVER WOULD HAVE guessed it was my biggest problem in church life, always thought we were so thoughtful, so capable of subtlety, we Presbyterians. But with more and more time way from the church, I'm becoming convinced that the rules are what hold us Christians back. What desire we have—for making laws out of poems, making absolute laws out of laws Jesus himself challenged. I don't mean hold us back from hedonism—it's clear I'll never have that in me: I mean hold us back from actual religious experience, one that can see the sacred in the world, God's Breath in all of creation. Yes, Father, I am aware of the self-serving dimension of questioning the rules after kissing Janey. But.

The rules hold us back so well because we don't even see them there behind it all. Solo fide, solo gratia, we say, as we live lives solely according to the safety of rules upon rules upon rules. We cleave to their comfort, even if they aren't the beauty that ever attracted us, cannot give life to sustain us and are unimaginable as an outgrowth from Christ. Thinking of Christ as a rule follower is nearly as ridiculous as thinking of him as conservative. And yet we are both those things. I wonder what you do with this. You're an intelligent man. It couldn't be that you read the Bible and see Christ approving of religious elitisms or advocating for preemptive war. Is Christ, in your secret theology, just the spark that ignited all the old conservative white American men to finally unradicalize and codify the faith, thank God? You've spoken to me about all good theology starting with the Baptists. Lord.

IV

36

In Jacob's House

I'VE ARRIVED IN PHOENIX. The familiar guilt of being in town without telling you has descended. It's strange: it's not that I think you want my company, it's that I know you'd resent that I don't want yours.

I stay with my old friend Jacob, his wife and four kids. What a good man he is, how faithful and kind, an elder in his church. News of me has spread to my old Phoenix friends who came to faith with me in the evangelical world. Jacob and I were baptized on the same night, at one of those rollicking affairs at Grace Bible, you'll recall. He and his family are good to take me in now, radioactive as I am.

When I arrive, Jacob is gone at work. It's just his wife, Janice there, an hour before she has to pick up the kids in a circuit around town.

She offers me coffee. We sit across from each other at their kitchen island. The silence is thick and I'm grateful she's attempting to tolerate it. She looks angry to me. I don't blame her. I'm angry with me too. I've failed not just my wife but all wives, let down the story, the extremely tenuous story, we tell ourselves about what Christian Marriage is. She also looks sad for me, scared of me.

"I don't really know what to talk about," she says.

"Sorry. Seen any good movies lately?"

She does not dig this joke.

"I don't expect you to embrace me. I don't understand what I'm going through well enough to defend it," I say.

"What about what Leah's going through." I exhale, nodding my head as I acknowledge the force of the blow.

"I am ashamed of leaving. I won't defend myself."

I manage to sit in this, looking her sadly in the eye.

"How are you," she asks.

"Kinda rough," I say. And her guardedness is gone in an instant. I'm suddenly no threat to her. God am I glad to encounter an evangelical faith tempered by femininity, if as likely to see me as wrong, more likely to attend to the hurt in front of her rather than locate and interrogate whatever part of me the wrong lives in.

When Jacob gets home he pours us bourbon; I'm grateful teetotalling has grown less common among Phoenix area evangelicals than it was in my days here. His easy kindness is overwhelming and genuine. I'd like to believe he knows he knows me, knows I haven't transgressed beyond the retaining walls that held his ole friend.

He's more willing than Janice to humor me with less weighty conversation as he fills me in on the political infighting of Sun Devil basketball as we watch them play on TV. Inside sports talk on a sport I haven't followed in twenty years is generally not my thing but listening to Jacob is nostalgic for me: I know I know him. His lack of judgment is a shock, probably because the judgmental ones got to me first, not because of who Jacob ever could be.

He does call a black man articulate as we watch a courtside interview. Unable to resist the now-parallel pulls of my Progressive Identity's truth and my evangelical need to convince others of my truth, I talk to him about it. He endures my lecturing and in a matter of a few sentences, he's able to humbly acknowledge the racism—his word—underlying the statement. How rare is his guilelessness. I hope I am as swayable when truth finds my presumptions. None of my Los Angeles people, all of whom would be aghast at that "articulate" line, have black children, which he and Janice do, three of their four children adopted, not because they couldn't have more children but because they wanted to live out their beliefs.

We get somewhat drunk as he shows me The Rock in 4k on his new AV setup, humoring some part of me I didn't know was there with updates from the gang of our old days in Fellowship of Christian Athletes and Young Life. There's exactly zero malice or gossip in it. You can smell the goodness on this man.

37

For Mom

Sleeping in Jacob's newly remodeled guest room, feeling safe, I've slowed down and holed up.

At the suggestion of a therapist friend of mine, I wrote Mom a letter after her death. It's been in the glove box of the Volvo, folded into the liner notes of an old CD. No matter what else goes into these pages, I imagine this will be the most vulnerable part of the whole wound.

～

Dear Ma,

We couldn't have a typical funeral. We had dinner and drinks in the private dining room of your beloved Stockyards, that old steakhouse with the paisley carpet—still smelling of cigarettes, decades illegal in Arizona restaurants.

I can see your giddy smile as we enter that place and they greet you by name. I inherited your smile but I haven't smiled as big, as unabashedly, as you would at even a small adult joy, since I was ten. I remember, shortly after my twenty-first birthday and a bad break up, you took me to the bar at Stockyards for a Manhattan. You had misplaced one earing, as you often did, and you looked like a pirate in a purple tennis jumpsuit, diamonds from your first marriage still dangling from one ear, on your ring finger, your old trusty Rolex.

"She was nice. I liked her," you said.

"I know, Ma."

"She'd get back together with you, if you wanted."

"Geez, Ma. What the hell?"

You looked at me sidelong.

"She tell you that," I asked.

You nodded coyly.

"I can't be the one to take care of her anymore," I said.

"Okay okay. I love you," you said.

Your turn toward love for me was as complete as it was sudden. It didn't matter that you were busy advocating for my poor dumped girlfriend a minute ago (but even this was an act of love, purer still that it was for the most damaged party, even over your son, for a moment).

I have a picture of us from that day, your smile gone wry as though you knew how funny your one gaudy earing looked, and liked it. In your leanest years, in which you borrowed thousands from me, a pastoral intern, you never gave in and sold your most precious pieces of jewelry. I'm sorry I was pragmatic and critical about it. I see the romantic idealism in it, the longing for the good old days you needed to keep at hand in the form of their relics. I see the way you occasionally, opulently, took care of yourself the way you did others in every moment you had. I am thinking especially here of the $10,000 hand blown crystal sculpture of a violin you bought on a trip to Milan at a time when you were underwater on your mortgage. You were ridiculous. And a wonder to me. All the ridicule has bled out from my wonder, all I didn't understand about you now just adornments dangling from your mystery.

In your life, your accomplishments in kindness were so vast they didn't line up beside your relational and professional failures, your retreat from friendships and, finally, your failure to resist your addiction and the pull of your own personal darkness. I call them failures not because I think of them that way but because I know you did. I believe others' perceptions of you as a failure became a pillar of your identity, one I wish I could have talked you out of.

A funeral in a church just didn't line up as a party we could honestly throw. As the pastor in the family, everyone deferred to me; they would neither make me preach your funeral nor engage a hired gun to sub in. I'm sorry; I know you would have wanted a formal affair with bygone friends lined up to pay their respects. I'm sorry I didn't have the fortitude to believe they'd show; I experienced what you did: the ole friends had abandoned you.

But now I wonder if I was wrong, swept away too far by the hopelessness in your death, that they would indeed have come out of the woodwork one last time for you, no matter the separation of years, geographical and emotional distance. I'm sorry I couldn't find a foothold in that hope for you.

A large dinner, sharing stories of the good and the pain around food and drink, was more tolerable for us than a small funeral, even if we were drinking booze, which killed you, in order to be strong enough, numb just enough, to get through it.

You were fondly remembered that night. Dad cried. "She was the most giving person I ever knew," he said. Wayne raised his glass and harrumphed a "here here" in response, the closest moment they ever shared.

I miss our kinship as the two emotional people in the family.

But I was just barely in your ballpark, your swings so much faster, between poles so much further apart than mine. Knowing something of despair and comparing your troughs to mine is an exercise in pity and guilt. What you could have been, with a little real help. With medication other than alcohol.

Ma, I can't think of your death as anything but a suicide. I know you thought, in your darkest moments—and how could weeks of round-the-clock drinking not be cut from your darkest cloth?—that you were mostly a burden on those that loved you, that leaving an inheritance gave you great comfort, that you were worried you'd blow through your money, itself recently inherited from Aunt Betty, before you died to leave it, that you had a life insurance policy that covered accidental death. For the record, "accidental" means slipping on a banana peel, not drinking yourself to death in a way that allows the examiner to label the cause organ failure.

*I don't think anyone else cares to stare into the abyss and name this hopelessness as I have—*suicide*—but it was a suicide, the shame of it, that we were all responding to by keeping the affair out of the church, out of any big public setting, me out of the pulpit.*

I say this not to further your shame, Ma, but to say I know all of you, know personally the desire to give in to despair, see forensically, in the state of your house and financial arrangements, that you gave in, and I love you beyond anything still. You were beautiful to me in every moment of your life, including the last ones. I am charmed by, enamored of, your misguided life insurance purchases, not heartbroken anymore.

I don't spend as much time blaming myself for not saving you as I did, early on. I don't know what changed, exactly, but I know the more compassion I've given you and what you were going through, as my grip on blame of and anger toward have slipped, I've been able to believe myself when I say, It's okay I didn't swoop in. *And if I'm gonna let myself off for not saving you, I've got to let you off for needing out.*

It's okay you couldn't go on, Ma.

You were quite a mess. But.

You showed me how to love unconditionally and there isn't another person in my life who's done that.

When we were packing up your house, after we'd walked through it with the estate sale lady, had gotten mementos for ourselves and our wives and kids, we walked out to the cars to go. James and I were anxious to move everyone away from the scene of the crime. Gus, just two and a half, waddled out last. James had just explained death to Gus, alone in your bedroom together, which he told me was the hardest parenting task of his life. On his way off the property, Gus took a turn, sat down in front of your closed garage door and crossed his arms in that stubborn tiny old man way he has.

"I'm not giving up," he said.

"What, buddy," James asked him.

He raised the elbows of his crossed arms head-high before slapping them back down on his belly and pushing his ass flush against the garage door.

"I'm not giving up!" On your resurrection, I guess.

James sat down with him and held him. We all just waited a few minutes, the wives walking to the other side of the SUVs to hide their crying, until little Gus was ready to stomp back to the car.

James' tough guy demeanor, which hadn't even cracked during his death explainer, melted as he cried his way back to the car, his eyes tilted up and away from Gus.

Mother, I'm gonna stop white knuckling this.

That feeling people have, that they need to release a loved one so they can stop being haunted by their ghost—I'm looking to stop haunting you, quit bothering over all that was undone and thank you for what was: you were a blazing success in all that mattered, an open bleeding heart of bottomless compassion and charity, and fuck this backward world that calls a woman like you a failure so often and exhaustively it could gaslight such an idealist into believing it. Goddamnit, you were not a failure, Ma, and I repent that I ever engaged the conversation in those terms, comforting you over the fact of your failures when I should've been raging against that upside down ascription.

I'm going to stop alternating between blaming you and blaming myself—it's a doubly false, and exhausting, story—and just not blame. One day.

I think of you every day. It has become so sweet, most days, no longer a wrestler in my gut that pulls me to the floor. You are now, mostly—it'll never be painless—a reverie, when I encounter a bird or a breeze or a smile you would have loved, not a grief, not a whisper of guilt. Thank you for being mine.

For Mom

∾

If you have anything critical to say about this letter, Father, I ask that you just text me "relationship over" instead.

38

Impossible Repair

I'VE BEEN READING TA-NAHISI Coates again. I'm embarrassed to say it's because I kissed Janey. I don't understand her experience as a black woman and so I'm reading a book. Old habits, forged in religion, die hard.

I'd be surprised if you, dear Self-Limiting One, knew who Coates was. I imagine some people on your outlets disparaged him at one point—he wrote an essay titled The Case for Reparations in 2014—but after one news cycle, I doubt he could compete with the slice of consciousness Barack Hussein Obama occupied. That essay happens to be beautifully written, elegantly reasoned and utterly persuasive. By telling you I find it persuasive, that the experience of African-Americans fills me with a deep sense of white culpability, I'm doing what Coates did with his essay's title—insuring you won't read on, hear on; you can't. And yet I still have the need, at this time in my life, to state it. If I were more clever, I'd first mention his more famous father-to-son work, Between the World and Me. But your defenses wouldn't allow it to penetrate either. Might as well strike out swinging for the fences.

It's disturbing to engage with the African-American experience. It feels unsafe to consider my own culpability in systems of oppression. It's further complicated because I too am a victim of you all, old white men. But it hasn't been my skin color that occasioned my abuse. My hurting—for not buying in and now for opting out—was at least eligible for a guilt experience, while the vitriol hurled upon black communities for their blackness is a plain message of shame (even when it masqueraded as hate for *behavior*, like laziness or criminality, and not hate for their very being, which of course it was and is). Maybe that's the difference between abuse and oppression. I have sympathy for whites who've had a hard time in life; when they confuse a weakening of their monopoly on cultural power with persecution that's when my big disagreements begin.

I know well the conservative instinct toward unsafety: you will push away hard feelings as threats, push away the truths of white culpability as lies, your son's acknowledgement of that culpability as weakness, even betrayal. Because these are all kneejerk reactions, they preclude the possibility of your ever even hearing The Other's experience, of ever reading on. This is tragic.

Thinking of the hopelessness of your transformation makes me desperately sad. Coates takes the long view. He reminds us that there were black abolitionists who died with multiple enslaved generations yet to come before emancipation and that our lifetimes might likewise lack completion.

I hope one day I'll have children. I believe I can work on a new identity of racial peace-making for my family. Is it just my Christian obsession with *redemption* that needs your racial ethic killed and re-embodied within you in the space of this one life?

39

Rant

GOOD GOD, IT'S HITTING the fan in America right now. Slowing down at Jacob's, I've had time to read news while ignoring my email and texts and, God help me, look at twitter. It's so strange to be unengaged and then come back to a news feed in this time, like sleeping through whole strata in the fossil record just to be whiplash telescoped back, to a view of each organism on the microscopic level, as its cells divide in time lapse. And to wonder what the strata will preserve—is this outrage, historical in any other time, impeachable in other times, even memorable from this one? To see senate hearings for your newest judge go on with a little bit less decorum, a bit more vociferous objection from the opposition, to see American *Democracy* keep churning despite the fact that this is all against the will of most of us, as the congressmen and senators in charge of the proceedings represent minority rule, is gaslighting in the extreme. To see white fragility transmigrate into white rage, as I so often did in my childhood with you, now on the face of your judge and his white knight senate defender, Lindsay Graham. Their sputtering faces remind me of yours, when you'd *had* it, when the time for reason was over and you were set to assert your furious will. I don't know what's more alarming: that it's all manufactured, a grotesque theatre piece, as I lean toward for Graham, or that all this snarling and crying—hysterically, we'd say, if he were a she—actually comes from an emotional reality, as I lean toward for Kavanaugh. Yes, it seems that he believes the possibility of the haulting of his assent to the highest possible position in American jurisprudence—for the paltry accusation of some light teenage sexual assault—represents an oppression.

Could you and yours please cut the shit?

How laughable has the "What if Democrats did what the Republicans are doing now?" test. What if Obama had transgressed beyond the wearing of a tan suit, and, say, cheated on his pregnant wife with a porn star months after their child was born and paid off that woman to keep silent, as well as other women, with what seems to amount to illegal campaign spending? Sir, your head would explode. Your sphincter would rupture.

Obama never could have become president, so pure did he have to be to compensate for his blackness, if he'd had but a single divorce in his past. His extraordinary marriage and relationship with his daughters can be credited as a lack of family values, somehow, just as his testified and lived Christian faith can be called Islam, just as his blackness can call his birth certificate into question. Trump's whiteness is credited as such purity, on the other hand, he can be more grotesque a figure than ever conjured in fiction and be championed by you and yours as God's own choice.

What is my generation to make of you? I was so long flabbergasted, fomenting within the church for fuller consideration of minority rights and congruent advocacy, dumbfounded that these concerns that seemed so clearly Jesus' to me weren't even on my leaders' radar. I somehow convinced myself simply raising the objection often enough and well enough would effect change. I feel so foolish for never having considered the simplest explanation, now the clearest, that white supremacy was the highest value in play. Coates is excellent on a related point: it's not that working class whites have been duped into voting against their interests on healthcare and taxation, as progressives are fond of saying, it's that they have, all along, held white supremacy as the higher value, and there's been one party catering to that value. To this point, merely with dog whistles. Now, with a megaphone. I'm sorry to sound so radical—I, raised by Midwesterners, long for conservativeness, of demeanor at least—but my generation must conclude it isn't the Christian God but White America's god you're talking about—and have been all along. I say this to my embarrassment; I say it hoping for the best-case scenario, that I was duped, and not the worst, that I was along for the ride.

My generation embraced purity, its volumes of rules, because you taught us these rules had meaning, that the good served by following them would be worth the arduous struggle. Build character. What character have you got, Father? What greed, to sniff out and rush hungrily toward whatever possible short-term payoffs you can manage while gerrymandered minority rule holds. You encouraged rule following only by those under your rule, so you could maintain the autonomy to set and break those rules. The end justifies the means for you, and—good God, Moral Majority; my stars, values voters—how hard is it to see that Machiavelli is as far from Christ as it gets? For Christ, the means—humility unto death on a cross— were the end. Again, I am sorry this sounds so radical, I am sure it will leave me unheard but I'm unable to mince any longer.

But do you even know what I'm talking about?

Have your outlets just been running stories on Hillary's child sex rings during all this? I've been drinking a lot of Jacob's espresso pods.

40

Wandering by Still Waters

I WAKE IN THE morning to Jacob asking if I want to go quail hunting.

"No."

"Just like in high school," he says.

"Yeah. No disrespect. Just can't."

"Well, it can wait a day," he says. "I got something else you'll like to see."

He gets me in the car and we get coffee from a Dutch Bros drive-thru windmill.

"I've been thinking about that facebook post of yours," he says.

"The text of my last sermon."

He laughs. "Really," he asks.

I nod.

"Dang. I would've loved to see that." He is smiling and laughing. "I want to take you to our church."

I'm shaking my head and making faces.

"Not for a service. I want you to see what we're doing," he says.

⁓

I remember this church, its carpet the deep green of schmaltz incapable of seriousness, let alone the most serious seriousness, the sacred. The green of the felt on an elf's hat.

It still smells of stale incense, a smell I couldn't place as an evangelical teen but loved. Now that I do recognize it, I'm confused, imagining some high-church rapscallions sneaking in in the dead of night for decades on end to visit liturgical mischief upon the denominationless.

I cry. After, I guess, this green has touched my visual cortex, when it and the stale incense/carpet glue scents get shipped to whatever in the brain holds memories of the sacred. God, I love The Church. It's hurt me so much, especially these evangelical spaces. But it hurts like home hurts. Nostalgia means little wound, which I learned in a book. If this is a wound it is in my mouth and it won't heal because I'll never stop tonging it. This metaphor I take from Fight Club. I am a white man from Arizona.

When Jacob introduces me to Romero, the undocumented refugee who's been staying at By Still Waters Bible Church, my categories take a hit half as great as when the people of my church shunned me. The idea of an evangelical church in Arizona being convicted of the need to take in the refugee gives me strength in a particularly Jacobian way. He never stopped seeking God's will for his life, which he construed not as some secret treasure map to be divined but as the way of the cross, the way toward greater sacrificial love. There will always be, I feel so strongly with Jacob, those whose Christ-consciousness drives them to greater and greater love of The (formerly) Other.

I mentioned my inheritance from my mother. You've said, a number of times, oh Withholding One, that I shouldn't expect anything from you as an inheritance. You've taught me scarcity my whole life and I've never asked for your money; I don't expect things to suddenly change in death. But knowing that you, whose lens for all interaction is transaction, whose primary language is money, needed to tell me that zero money would ever be coming, it sounded like you just wanted to make sure I knew I was un-loved in case there was any lingering doubt. Truly, I don't want it—I also think your giving it all away would instantly make you happier. But when you tell me I'm not worth your only currency, how could you not see this speaks my worthlessness in your eyes?

Let me be crass. My mother left me about $100,000, a sum that blows my mind and would change my life, a sum that can immediately erase my seminary loans, or hell, front a down payment for a decrepit shack in LA. If I had a job to qualify for a loan. It's how I'm wandering now without threat of financial collapse. Wayne, in that frontiersman accent and cadence of his, pronounced wandering like wondering and wondering like wander-ing. I'm doing both. I'm doing either. He and the other cowboys I grew up around, the Reservation Indians I spent time with on the missions trips that gave me life then and make me cringe now, who spoke with a lilt not dissimilar, a two-way linguistic influence, I imagine, cowboys and Indians, Indians and cowboys, they all knew in their language whether or not they knew they knew. We're doing both. We're doing either.

I have no real concept of your finances, Father. But I can't imagine that $100,000 is any more than a tenth of what you could burn tomorrow with no real impact on your life. Again, I don't want it; please do burn it. I'm not trying to talk you into a different attitude regarding me and your dollars, I'm positing a different understanding of relationship.

"Mucho gusto," I say, as I meet Romero.

"You know Jacob," he asks.

"Since we were niñitos," I say.

"He is a good man," Romero says. "A family man."

Romero's wife and two children, all citizens, live a couple miles away, coming to the church every morning and afternoon to visit him and play on the church's playground. Romero had lived and worked in Phoenix fifteen years before ICE ever had the mandate or the gall to go after him. He lived here back when Sheriff Joe Arpaio himself thought undocumented immigrants weren't committing crimes worth prosecuting.

It reminds me what a strange thing it is to tell people I'm from Arizona, to make excuses for the way it used to be, the natural beauty right there in North Scottsdale, now tract homes, the now dead conservatism of Goldwater, which was still insane, don't get me wrong, but charmingly so, to me at least, which accepted the mutual needs of Mexican American workers and American farm owners, did not pathologize brown skin, quite so completely at least. I simply don't recognize the place anymore. But I see I've changed too.

Romero has me thinking of inheritance because he has me thinking of *money* and *deserve*. I want to leave him a few thousand of these dollars freely gifted to me. This is my mom in me. I leave him a hundred—the mom in me attenuated by the you in me, the Pastor Steve in me, The Church in me. I exit the church quickly after palming Romero the money, unable to look at him and receive the way he'll receive.

41

Pastoring Against Type

A FEW MONTHS BEFORE I left the subchurch, shortly after your lecture on the morality of pastoring the *kinds* of people I did, Brian, an actor, came to me shaking, deeply frightened of his experience of acting. He was relatively successful, getting consistent guest parts and multi-episode arcs on TV shows. He was newly married. I presumed he was having trouble with kissing other women on screen, as I'd seen him do. I'd worried about him coming to discuss it with me. The kissing made me extremely uncomfortable and I had no idea how I was going to work with him. My purity frameworks still operant, I couldn't imagine how to tell him that he could, should—or how to—work through it; I also knew I didn't understand his work well enough to condemn it. Not that condemnation was ever something I saw as a part of ministry.

"What is it," I asked him.

"The violence is getting to me. I've played three killers in a row. In four weeks. And there's one more episode on this one. It's the most successful string of work I've ever had," he said, laughing nervously.

"I don't think I understand. It's fake—choreographed—isn't it?"

He shook his head quickly, wobbly at the neck as if from a concurrent chill, as if to shake out my notion as an earworm in his own skull. "There's no way to fake-strangle someone. You gotta put your hands around another human being's neck and squeeze."

I nodded grimly, managing not to say "Dayum" out loud, as I took in this heretofore unknown level of goth from Brian.

"The guns aren't so bad. But either way, if it's a murder scene, you're connecting to anger, to . . . beyond anger—to hate and pushing that out through your fingers, out onto their skin, skin that covers a throbbing artery. If your hands are around another person's neck."

"It seems like you've thought about this a good deal."

Brian broke down. I hugged him.

"I don't want to feel that hate. I can't believe it's what God wants for me and my work."

"Maybe we should take some time after you're done with this gig, to think about your values and how to apply them. Can you get through this part? Do you want to?"

"Yeah, I can. I want to."

"Okay."

"I wonder what it's worth," Brian said, motorboating his lips on a sigh. "What my work on fuckin crime shows for an audience of 60-year-olds is accomplishing."

I took a breath, trying to decide if I wanted to say this next thing.

"Would you like to know what I think of your work?"

"Yes," he said to me, fragile desperation in his eyes. I felt the power I had to devastate him with my withholding or with my approval, the power we've somehow seen fit to vest in pastors.

"I think your work is beautiful. Even on shows I think are horrible. I've seen in your face, on my TV screen, the pain you're talking about now. Your killers aren't monsters; they're people with a past that bent them this way. Even when the writers haven't done the job of putting that history in them, I see it on you."

How rare it is to be invited to share your love of someone with them, your blessing over them, how wonderful to grasp in the dark for the right words and find you've laid your hand right on them.

He looked at me in disbelief, a look of hesitation over accepting a compliment, harder still for its extravagance. Did he get here the way I did, self-criticism engrained from age zero, the instinct to make a show of your self-flagellation over a missed goal in youth soccer carried through to "I could've done better" even in teenage successes, in an unbroken chain all the way into your adult doubts over your life's work? Who are we performing this for now? Our fathers and coaches are long gone. But of course we Christians have found pastors to keep the position filled. Was my playing the role of pastor against type, refusing to affirm his self-doubt, destabilizing for him? Was he asking, as I see I have of pastors and *accountability partners,* "Dose me the shame, please?"

"Remember when you played the child rapist and murderer in that play? I'll never forget the journey you took the audience on. From disgust to compassion—what an arc," I said.

He was weeping by this point, looking at me with the wet eyes of a son finally stamped worthy. How I could have abused this terrible power, say, if I'd just started in on my doubts about kissing non-wives.

"I thought kissing other women would be the hard part after I got married," he said. I wonder if my gulp was audible.

"Is that hard?"

"In ways I didn't expect. It's always Sherry, that I'm leaving in the morning, coming home to, and thinking about in a *love* scene. If it bothered her, I'd stop. She trusts me completely. And *that* is the scary part. But what's a kiss. It's an act of connection, of compassion. It isn't a movement up into the highest parts of me, and I stop it if that feels like the threat. And it isn't a descent into hate, like violent scenes."

How warped are my categories. How did we American Christians get here, fencing off love related *sins* while shrugging off the hate related ones. A naked body is more frightening to us than a dismembered one.

42

Blood

I NEVER DREAM ABOUT my mother. I think of her all the time in waking life, am haunted by those hospital images. Far less often than they used to, they still arise out of nowhere, in the middle of doing dishes or driving some-where, and grab hold of me, curling all of me in toward my contracting gut. So much blood—it wouldn't clot—that they had draining tubes down her nose and mouth to constantly suck it up. The tape they used to stick the tubes in place was red with her watery blood, despite their constant changing. She wouldn't clot so she was losing blood, so they were pumping her full of blood, which oozed back out because she wouldn't clot. I think of the blood on her face all the time, her veined cheeks purple and red, her permatanned skin so pale. Somehow it doesn't haunt my dreams. I dream of you, Father, often.

43

Guns Guns Guns

THE GUNS. DEAR GOD, the guns. The shootings in America just keep happening, their horror grown so mundane. I've been thinking about gun ownership very much lately, have had to work to push away the impulse—bred into me or imbued by my frontiersmen father figures—to stockpile. I've always tried to *be the change* and all that, and believing America would be better with fewer guns, never been a collector. Always kept the one pistol gifted to me hidden away, from myself, from others. But it's become quite hard, Father, to imagine your side giving in to democracy rather than the loss of a civil war, so entrenched are you, oh Zealous One.

That pistol is tucked away, in its zipper case, in my car trunk now, bound for a return.

I'm questioning that return, like all things. If your side refuses to let go of its terms for any debate, must we not at some point engage on those terms? Can't bring knives to a gun fight. If that's true rhetorically, is it not true actually, at some final, literal last gasp from your side? Your guns are actual.

Not to fear. I know I don't have it in me to keep even this one little pistol, its mere low-capacity magazine. I've taken all that turn the other cheek business quite literally for decades now. Even the manifold hypocrisy of my teachers can't just disappear it.

44

Location Sharing

I WALK INTO A Trader Joes to get some food, the one in the fanciest part of Scottsdale, quite near where you've lived for years now. I risk it only because you've told me you only shop at Whole Foods and Sprouts. It's a very small store and I like it because it's rarely busy. I walk through the door and there you are, Father, ten yards away, inspecting an avocado. As your eyes move up from the avocado, perhaps toward me, I turn and run out the building. Maybe one day, I'll ask if you saw me or thought *that fellow's head looks like John's* or have no idea whatsoever about it.

When I get outside, Salt calls my name from his Corolla. I am shocked and relieved. He is tentative, waiting on some kind of criticism from me, it seems. But I run to his car and get in.

"Drive, please. Please drive," I say. And he does. "Pull over," I say, after we've made it a few blocks.

"Leah's password was her birthday," he says, apologetically. "You've got location sharing on with her."

I nod. Woe for the days of smartphoneless absconding.

"Her parents send you," I ask him.

"They offered me money but I didn't take it. They don't know I'm here. I'm here for me."

"Okay," I say, reaching out and awkwardly hugging him as he drives. "Shit," I say, remembering I've got to move the Volvo before you see it in the Trader Joes parking lot.

～

Salt and I sit in the Volvo, in the drive through at Aliberto's. Salt is from Tucson, meaning Arizona style burritos, unblighted by rice, have always been a touchstone for us.

"Arcade Fire's playing in Vegas tonight, wanna go" Salt says.

"Oh," I exhale, as my mind catapults me out of the present.

Hearing the band's name in Arizona, as I haven't in a decade, first sends me to a moment in 2005 when I heard Wake Up in an Irish sports bar in Tucson and thought, okay now they've *made it*, before punting me seventeen years back, seventeen years it's been that I've known Will Butler of Arcade Fire.

It doesn't fit, it's intrusive, picturing Will here and now. We bonded tightly in college and have been close since but have talked less and less over the past couple years, haven't talked at all in months—talking on the phone has grown arduous, his success a sludgy mote between us these few years my upward professional ascent has been clearly kyboshed—haven't talked since before I left my church and wife. He was always insulated from my LA church life, no mutual connections; he must not know a thing about where I'm at.

It's strange and uncomfortable to claim our friendship with anyone, especially you, Father, the one who taught me hyper-vigilance in my self-monitoring for boasting. This monitoring applies at least doubly to claims of association as association is the opposite of accomplishment, self-madeness one of your, and thus my, myths of choice. But I claim my friend—despite the hanger-on discomfort, despite the queasiness of how he'd think of it and despite how pathetic it makes me feel sometimes that I'm proud I know him.

The context in which Will and I formed our friendship seems like a moon to the planet I've lived on since, a moon spinning out of its orbit after the recent cataclysms in my world. I was his resident advisor in college. We'd talked Talking Heads and Suicide and Neutral Milk Hotel, felt bonded over our outsider positions within our outsider faith systems—an outsiderness keenly felt at that liberal bastion you so despise—my evangelicalism and his Mormonism. Not that I share your conceptions, but it was odd to take writing and art classes there, be respected in them until my peers found out I was into Jesus, at which point I wasn't ostracized, wasn't persecuted, no, but felt a bit suspect, like a double agent.

"This is my brother, Win's, band," he said, a month into our friendship, CD-R in nervous hand as he stood outside my palatial R.A.'s suite.

At Northwestern, Will was far from the band's Montreal hub. His self-monitoring over claims on the band the one vigilantly operating then, he didn't say he was a member of the band. This despite having played on the recordings he held in his hand, a fact I didn't learn until weeks later.

I was a deejay at the radio station by then, which is why he was foisting this disc. I tried to temper any airplay hopes he might have had because, well, when has your friend's brother's band ever been good? But.

Before the first track was through on that collection of shitty recordings, captured by some dude holding up a DAT recorder at live shows, I knew there was something for me and my people to worry over long and love well. Such sweet weirdness in *Goodnight Boy,* where in a dream sung by Win, a father must quiet his handicapped son, both hiding in an attic, to keep them from being discovered by a mob: "*Good night, boy, go to sleep boy, shut up boy, for me,*" he sings with terrible care. The father is of course the damn town mayor because from the beginning through to now in Arcade Fire's mythology, it's all always been about *the neighborhood.* That's the closest thing to a chorus that song's got, and chorus it does, lullabying again and again across the jangly arrangement. The ache of these songs, of growing up confused, latchkey lonely and overwrought in the suburbs, was here in stronger dose than on their later record, The Suburbs, the manic hunger of chasing a crush across multiple states on a late night drive (*Headlights Look Like Diamonds*), the confessional brother-to-brother regret of *William Pierce*, sung by Win to his younger brother, my new younger friend, and what is an RA but a ham-fisted attempt at institutionalizing sibling guidance—that in my case somehow took, as he became my best friend.

By five tracks in, I was convinced this band was going to make a dent on the globe, even a dent measured in dollars—no mere Velvet Underground *influence* for them—a feat I expected from about zero bands I loved. It was artsy-fartsy but with a novel, broad and powerful appeal, the kind of weirdo music that can pierce, by virtue of talent, will and the grand luck of timing, The Main Stream. The Flaming Lips, whose Soft Bulletin had moved me and my people just a couple years prior—were the best analogue I could name for the kind of success I dreamed for them in the days after I finished my first listen of that CD-R. I undershot it by a piece; it was only a few years before The Flaming Lips were playing beneath them at music festivals, Wayne Coyne, The Lips' gray-bearded singer, starting childish aesthetic/ethical debates with young Win.

IV

I was a fanboy immediately, more than tolerated by the band, I like to think, tagging along to those early shows in Montreal when Will was on breaks from school. The EP release show, I remember, Spring Break 2003, furiously folding liner notes for CD sales at the show, our insides humming at whatever debut this EP meant, sleeping on flopped a mattress in Win and Brendan's shitty apartment, smelling of Pilsners, above that horrible bar, only to have the band "break up" mid-release show, when Brendan, the drummer then, started throwing toms at Win's head.

Brendan had missed his cue on a song.

"You're doing it wrong! You're doing it wrong," Win turned and screamed at him. I took Win to be 65% joking. Brendan seemed to think he was at least 80% serious. Thus the tom-tom throwing, the relationship severing, the "break up."

I put them on the air the week Will handed me that disc, which must make me the first American deejay to play Arcade Fire. I think Win had gotten somebody at his art school to play it in Montreal by then but I can't imagine a CD-R had been family-line smuggled to another American before me. I wish I could remember what track.

This claiming the touch of the hem of fame's garment now has me nauseous. I imagine my reaction is only a mirror of yours. The you in me tells me to be envious of my friend's success, which I certainly am, and also disdainful of fame over such a trifle—rock music. I don't believe art is a trifle; I celebrate their fame while despising my envy. But celebrating it while something ingrained in me rears back, tells me I should be judging it, well, if that isn't exactly judgmental, isn't disgust directed outward, it certainly is a cyclone in my own gut.

In real life, I've long avoided mentioning my friendship with Will. We were equals; we were in art classes together, in a short-lived band together, each adored by professors and peers, each expected to do Big Things. It's false to say my discomfort is all born of modesty. Acknowledging his fame points out my failure. I realize we're in different lines of work but if I couldn't manage to Billy Graham the thing, I could've at least been the number two preacher at my Hollywood church, no? Be celebrated as pretty darn woke as Reformed pastors go, no? No.

I want to justify myself to myself, and to Will, tell him it ain't so easy to make it in preaching if you honor how you treat others in your community over your own advancements. But that conversation sounds quite pathetic to the success fetishist in me. And then I want to laugh at myself for ever wanting to *make it* in preaching, that I confused pastoring and preaching, God and my categories for God, that I could be so askew for so long. But I also just want to retreat, into those heady early days at Northwestern, or less early and headier yet in Montreal, or up on a damn cloud later, at their first show in Los Angeles at Spaceland—where I'd driven at eighty across town to make it just in time, coming from preaching my first sermon at seminary, my own performance praised by my heroes of the craft—watching Beck turned away at the door while my name was on that golden List, and this too has gone strange, its meaning then indecipherable through the lens of now, as Beck has also been demoted to playing beneath Arcade Fire, as long ago as Coachella 2014. But then, in 2004, to children of the 90s in his hometown of Silver Lake, Beck was big as Bono on The Cross.

On a night like that, then, to them and even to me, what in life and career couldn't be won?

"I'll text Will's assistant for passes," I say to Salt.

"They became roadtrip burritos," he giggles.

V

45

Hoover Damn

"Thank you. It's been a very good rest," I say to Jacob and Janice, eye contact too great a feat. "But I want to keep moving, I think."

Janice reaches out and tilts my chin up with her forefinger, some gesture she's mothered a hundred times, and when I look up to each of them I see warm smiles that want me to get what I need, not whatever disapproval of my wandering ways I'd anticipated.

Salt and I drive fast to Vegas. He connects his old ipod to the stereo, choosing to blare Neutral Milk Hotel, first Aeroplane, then the bootlegs. Salt is a quiet dude and this space where I have an even smaller desire to talk than he does is a rare one. I can tell he's decided to care for me and leave me be.

We're nearly to the Hoover Dam before Salt says, "I'm glad you wanted to go."

I'm glad too.

Now done with On Avery Island and thus all of Neutral Milk's canon and apocrypha, Salt click wheels through to that piano tinkling on Neighborhood #1—the first track on Arcade Fire's Funeral.

"No thanks," I say, before the churning guitar even breaks in.

"Ah, saving it," he says.

"Yes," I lie. In company, I don't care to be transported to the good ole days, before I was fundamentally a disappointment to myself, when the band's assent and mine were both positively inclined, even if not at parallel slope, when I would listen to this record all the way through and dream, at least, parallel dreams.

V

Salt puts on Johnny Cash as we sail past the Hoover Dam. What had been a clear sky is now streaked with clouds, in time to give us a properly stratified desert sunset as we enter Nevada.

∿

I remember flying to Phoenix to be at my mother's deathbed. On an early morning flight, the sunrise invisible until we'd ascended. The cloud cover was two-tiered, a contiguous blanket down over the ocean and wispy sheet out above, pink morning breaching the space between. I cry a lot on planes; I have a bad habit of reading poetry on them and the elevation alone has always gotten to me. Is that a thing? It feels like one. This proclivity and the sunrise had me taking to Instagram, captioning my sunrise image, "Beauty abounds. It never doesn't." I was on my way to my mother's hospital bed death, that death the product of her suicide by drink, a death, by smothering, of hope.

In my life, has gratitude ever been anything but a kneejerk defense? Against the frightening possibility that hope is indeed dead. I miss my step-father. A year after my mother's death, I told him via voicemail I couldn't take his phone calls any longer, that I was willing to pursue forgiveness and reconciliation, that I still loved him but that conversations that wholly avoided his role in my mother's addiction and death weren't possible. It's been another year, I haven't heard back and don't think I will. I don't know what he wanted from me, why he so consistently called to tell me of his love and support, his unwavering belief that I'd *make it*—he always framed my move to LA as a bold and glitzy one. He listened to, and enthusiastically gave notes on, every one of my podcasted sermons, which you, my *believing* father, never did. He was a dedicated unbeliever ("I don't *want* God's forgiveness" [also goth AF]). He gave me, without my chasing, the compassion I never had from you. Even if served alongside horrid shit. I don't know what in a son he chased in me but I did, in the end, withhold it. Perhaps, whatever your and my differences in substance, we aren't so different in style.

∿

I see no less faith in Ta-Nahisi Coates's black atheism, or Sherman Alexie's indigenous atheism, than in my, or your, Christian faith. No less beauty, the wounds they exhume in their writers' corners as holy a prayer as any I've offered. Their revenanting the multitude of griefs in life a pilgrimage I don't have the knees for. I think they might hate this. Alexie recounts the white woundings of his teenage friends saying "I don't really think of you as an Indian." Just as this bullshit keeps his friends from actually knowing him, my understanding of his and Coates' atheism as spiritual may occlude some of the truth they have for me. Any truth is embodied, theirs in bodies with color, without religion. But they aren't my audience here. My concern is the prayerlessness in our prayers, the faithlessness in our faith.

46

Festival

THE VEGAS SHOW IS at a music festival downtown, grubby burnout Vegas. At some unlikely moment since I was last here, we millenials covered it in six-story tall murals and gastropubs. And so downtown now seems okay by me, the sort of place I could inhabit for more than a night. It's a music festival; I know I shouldn't trust the sheen of a town lit by carnival lights but still it feels like it might stay cool, even after the circus has left town.

After we've picked up our passes from the organizers, Salt and I walk the midway, taking in the art installations. It is a breezy Fall night, still in the low 90s, dry as always, as we observe the kids—what in the world is it to grow up in Las Vegas?—and the music—Bastille (too white), Santigold (not white enough), festival crowds so strange to a dingy rock club kid like me.

"Man. Man, Maaan" Salt keeps saying. This is how he communicates excitement.

By the time we settle in for Arcade Fire's set, we're lit on a cloud of free coffee and *signature cocktails* from the artists' lounge, which, like all artists' lounges, contains only us hangers on, staring hungrily at other hangers on, a hunger without even the adjacent sating of an LA artists' lounge—no spare Galifianakis here or Paltrow there. No matter, Salt and I have and enjoy each another's company. And the fall desert air is a barometric home to us both.

Arcade Fire starts their set with Neighborhood #1 and Salt smiles at me—he's gotten his way, this the song I stopped in the car to halt the album. By the time they play Une annee sans lumiere, the third song of the set, the third song on Funeral, it's clear they're going to play the whole album.

I don't know if I'm ready for this and when Neighborhood #3 (Power Out) plays, I'm sure I'm not. I leave Salt and walk to the back of the crowd, sit down on the pavement and weep, as I am sent back to fourteen years ago, when this record was new, when our adult lives were new, *thumping* that shit out of the Volvo on my seminary campus proud—of them, and yes, of my connection to them, before they were *too* big a deal and I too small, when the pride was at least wrapped in, if not obliterated by, shame. There is so much shame. As I sit on this pavement, washed in this sound, as they plow through Funeral without a word between songs. How nice some banter would be, some of Win's Trump trash talk or a damn *hello* to dilute this dose but no, he knows exactly the power of this thing for us kids, this artifact brought to life, and he won't slow the rush once the release has begun, this power withheld over a decade now, a power, I imagine, the band was afraid to touch too. They must have walked around this relic dozens of times over the years before grasping it.

Fourteen years, put into a church, friendships, a marriage, all of it gone and irrecoverable. Worse than irrecoverable, a path I wish, for my and everyone's sake, I'd never stepped down.

Is all regret shame? Or just when it wet blankets you?

They play and play and play and play this power out, through the 40 foot speaker stacks, a power rated at 9.7. I was always confounded by what others saw in Funeral, the album, always found its engineering or production or whatever the hell hollow compared to how I knew them and these Funeral songs played live. But would Aeroplane, if I'd heard it for the first time out of a broke-ass tape deck, have floored me any less completely? No, Funeral was the good junk, to all us kids who heard it, no matter how.

9.7. That's what launched them, *our* music site, small enough to belong to us kids and big enough to be gospel, its pronouncements severe and infallible, its longed for approvals only ever measured and withholding—Pitchfork, a god we never expected to deign to even review the record, at least not so soon after release, did not review it so much as herald it, assigning it that 9.7 rating, a numerical value interpretable as THIS IS MY SON, WHOM I LOVE, LISTEN TO HIM, and labeled the infant band, in the final word of the text that unnecessarily adorned that 9.7—*arrived*.

The graphics of the stage show are twirling behind the band hypnotically, baroque woodcut inky drawings as from the cover art of the record, spinning into each other endlessly. Somehow it isn't until now that I think, I think and I remember—I must have been trying not to—In the Aeroplane

Over the Sea as an influence on all in this, even the visuals now twirling. It isn't until now that I remember those earliest days, as we stuffed copies of the EP in Win's Montreal shithole, us all agreeing that all of the lyrics from all of the songs on any record must be written together into one sentence, yes yes, as in the liner notes to Aeroplane. In the days of that EP release show, Arcade Fire still had a singing saw in the band, a musical influence so self-consciously Neutral Milk it had to be removed once the band became more its own. It isn't until now that I see this whole record as of a piece with that one. They are the two records for us kids. I've been listening to Aeroplane to avoid listening to Funeral; I've been listening to Aeroplane as a way of listening to Funeral. It's been playing all these notes of grief in me, as scales played in practice, preparing me for the grief of this performance, of the songs of the funeral itself. That's why I'm weeping.

Or rather, have wept, because now, overcome by beauty and gratitude, I am smiling and nodding, my head agreeing with some sentiment of my chest. I somehow got to be around for this second record. All us kids chasing Jeff Mangum, captain of Neutral Milk Hotel, like he was J.D. Salinger, and him avoiding us, leaving us, leaving recording and playing shows, like he was J.D. Salinger. While I got to be there for this second birth, and even the rearing of it, these fourteen years, allowed in—not completely, no, some distance must be maintained when fame comes in like a gargoyle lurking—but not shut out, these famous and fabulous artists still humans, still knowable, somewhat, not, like Mangum, reclusing himself from all us kids.

I am walking back toward the stage now, my body lighting up, as Wake Up begins. I am pushing my way through stacked bodies, laying aside my ever-present self-monitoring for impoliteness, back to Salt, back to the spot we'd staked out at the barricade in front of the stage. I don't respond to Salt's "Where'd you go?" I am dancing. Will has gone on a walkabout between the barricades separating sections of the crowd, a walkabout with a drum on a strap, which he beats the hell out of, as he marches and screams. Some version of this routine has been part of their show since I can remember. And it hasn't gotten old. He's good at his job and this is all clearly a fun time for him. His marching and wheeling has me back at the first time the band played Coachella, in 2005, the new It Band coming up against that arms-folded crowd of Angelinos. I remember, over the course of that set, how they multiplied the loaves with their magic, pulled that thin and long mass of a crowd into a thick and dense, and yet twice as long, lump, as their shouting sounds pulled bodies from adjacent stages, as Will climbed the lighting tower within his drummer boy routine. He doesn't climb lighting towers anymore. We are old.

By the time Rebellion (Lies) hits, we the crowd are in a reverie that feels like church. My least heavy, earliest experiences of church. And Will is yanking me over the barrier. Salt is helping him by pushing me up by the ass. And I am on Will's shoulders as he spins me around, waving off the security, who think I've done this of my own accord, as subtly as possible so as not to disturb whatever theater piece dances in his head. Will sets me down on the stage itself now, at which point it seems he thinks I'll be on my way but instead I yank at his drum and we drum together before I jump him and try to wrestle him to the ground. It's embarrassing my weight is no longer enough to get that job done. I go tingly knowing I've lost myself enough to dance, to play, to fight. Finally, Will pushes me in the back toward the wings of the stage and I take this cue, I go back to spectating.

The after party is in a classier downtown casino bar, the El Cortez, which is to say somewhat shitholey. I order rounds and rounds of liquers intended to punish—Jagermeister, Fireball, Rumchata—cocktail waitressing them around the room on a giant tray myself as we all dance like hell, as I, and Will and Win and the other husbands, whose wives are asleep or gone, dance, slowly inching away from the encroaching single ladies and back toward one another. The bar is a strange mix of invited guests of the band and randos Win and others have pulled of the damn casino floor in some demonstration of incognito largesse (if there is a crowd who won't recognize Arcade Fire by sight, it's those gambling at the El Cortez at 2am on a Monday).

But one of those randos pulled in is a young lady who has heard whose after-party this is. "I know who you are," she whispers to Salt as they dance. He shrugs performatively, which gets him the laugh of the night, me and Will and Win as amused by his charlatanism as he is. We, children of prudish religious systems and long-married, never got so much as a few dances out of the band's burgeoning name recognition or, in my case, hanger-on status. Good for him, selling borrowed stock high, seems to be the collective sentiment.

The night is wondrously full of good cheer. It never gets weird, despite the melancholy streak among each of us, factor-multiplied when all together, that streak inhibited, I think, by the constant and drowning Afro-Cuban beats coming out of the deejay booth. I never consider catching my ole friend Will up on my actual life. All is well as we say our goodnights around the party, all is well as I—now clearly drunk to myself in the absence of the party music—say goodnight to my ole friend at the cab stand, not even then feeling the temptation of some catharsis of close-ended confession, all is well as we shuttle back to our respective rock star or shitty ass hotel rooms, all is well up through when Salt and I leave hungover in the morning after three hours of sleep, getting drugs from Starbucks, when a pudgy bald man gets in a shouting match across the store with a tired looking woman in a halter top. They push each other, shouting, and, as I am waking from my stupor to ponder intervening, the woman peacocks her chest and says, "You wanna see my breast," and pulls out her breast.

On the way out, the interpretation of their indecipherable prior shouting that sticks with me is that the man must have been questioning her bonafides as a woman, to which questioning she responded with a breast. Vegas has finally come, crashing back down, into being Vegas, if only on the way out of town.

47

Wawasee

WE HAD SEX IN the shower at Lake Wawasee. That lake was a special place to you, Father, chosen for that and that it wasn't too far from James' home in Indianapolis. It was the first family vacation Leah had been on and the last time you attempted one, so terrible were the results. This was the phase of your relationship with your current wife where, it seemed to me, you coped with your wife's crazy by defining it as the new sane, when you were so full of hot anger it sweat out of you, not the cooler grieving sadness of you now, where you feel, even if you cannot name, something wrong under the skin. That week was our family's patented brand of anxious operating rules undivinable to an outsider like Leah—and, ever-shifting, to me too.

Being slapped into our family machine for five days, seeing the way its gears slipped and grinded, my wife was somehow turned on like never before, and we had sex in the shower at Lake Wawasee.

Your wife tried to bond with Leah one night, told her a side of the Spanking Story I'd never heard. According to your wife, you thought I was a perfect child before I was a troublesome teen—this is my memory too—when I voiced my disjunction with you, not in bad behavior but, having become a Christian, in ideological terms ("Father, I despise your world-view"). I know you hate the education I got at Northwestern. I've heard you lament the liberal warping I received. This has always mystified me. Our arguments were never greater than in my early teens and when we argued in my college years, my footing remained in my early teenage foothold, in Jesus. It was Christ and his love, liberally applied, that had me at odds with you, not a liberal conspiracy that stole me away. But of course, I see how that story can't be the one you tell yourself.

But the Spanking Story. Your wife told Leah that you spanked James all the time and it had begun to worry you that by the time I'd reached eight or nine you hadn't spanked me yet. You began *looking* for an infraction to occasion a spanking, she said, *made up* a reason to whack my bare ass—with that book on great white sharks, my favorite, I remember. I asked to pick the book. It was of coffee table book proportions, tall and wide, but not so thick as to complicate grip. I picked it to prove something. Not some tough guy fuck you—I was still a damn cherub, in the photos and in our memories—but that I agreed: I *had* done something terrible. How could I have thought otherwise? I trusted completely, as cherubs do. Your wife told Leah you cried when you confessed to this, that if she'd ever seen you cry—and she couldn't name another time—it'd never been like you cried when you admitted this.

How you regret, it seems, the way you treated me. In at least this instance. Of course you never confessed this to me. Here I've been, all this time, thinking I must have done something, at least some little thing, to *deserve* your violence. And yet I'm grateful to know it. Able to see some measure of grace in the great cost of even your partial confession, your nonprivate tears.

But we had sex in the shower at Lake Wawasee. It was after Leah and I stayed up playing Cards Against Humanity with James and his wife. James became so competitive, his fury incrementally rising at the thought that we were playing the game *wrong*, conspiring against his rightful victory, that he finally threw his cards at me and stomped out of the room. Leah often teased me about my competitiveness and my temper but James' response was a far sight beyond what she'd seen in me. She laughed loudly, thinking it was a performance, before flushing red and putting a flustered hand over her chest, a gesture not only of embarrassment, but of apology to James' wife for exacerbating the fallout by laughing.

There was another game there, at Lake Wawasee. Chess between me and your then eight-year-old son, Kyle. I've kept him out of this account; he doesn't deserve to be a tool, for good or for ill, in our discussion. He is turning into an amazing young man. But damn his cheating pissed me off. I admit, I was also pissed off by the years of provisions, of any expense, for his upbringing, for his private school and private tutors and private coaches, as I struggled to bring The Word to Los Angeles, a goal I thought you and

I shared. This feeling feels very petty to me but it is true. I knew many starving artists, none who struggled without asking for and/or receiving material support from their parents. None of these parents, I think, had anything like your material wealth. Yes, I know that part of the reason I tried to correct Kyle's cheating at chess was that I felt cheated, wanted my father to be less withholding in any regard, even in the crass realm of material provision. But I did try to correct him kindly and gently. It's not his fault he was born to you.

The other part of why I tried to correct him, I think, is that you didn't let me break a rule since the age of three; I simply had no rubric for such an allowance as you apparently now believed in for this child. But Good God did you and your wife lose your minds over my gentle suggestions that he not cheat up and down the board, as you turned my response to his behavior into something monstrous, some grand conspiracy against his *rights*. Leah was again stunned, unable to reconcile my family's responses, as though I had tortured the boy with a hunting knife, with what she saw with her eyes. This strikes me as a particularly germane form of gaslighting—reflexive nuclear level aggrievedness toward any suggestion of imperfection in you and yours. Yes, you went full Kavanaugh on me. So much more hurtful because here I am defined out of the category of you and yours, othered by my own blood.

But. We had sex in the shower at Lake Wawasee. She pulled me in, at noon, hungry for me like I'd never seen, hungry for me like in movies, with the teenage lust I'd never actually seen expressed as a teenager, my evangelicalism taking hold just before my sexual opportunities, and we had sex in the shower at Lake Wawasee. It must have been seeing the contrast between the men I was slated to become—you or my brother—and what she had in the actual product of me. I'm not so lovely out there in the world on my own, full of shame and sadness, of so much internalized hurt ready to bleed off of me and onto her caregiving hands—but next to you two? I am a saint of sacrificial love.

48

Extra Las Vegas

JAMES CALLS ME AND I pick up. It's been two years since his PR empire outgrew Indianapolis and he moved to Las Vegas, a four hour drive from me, a drive he hasn't made. I haven't either, to be fair. His job, as far as I can tell, is getting heads of companies drunk on golf courses and in casinos and so Las Vegas was a logical move. He's probably called me six times in that two years and yet he calls me now, when I'm in Vegas.

"Hey," he says.

"I'm in Vegas now," I tell him, defusing at least my geographical surprise; his calling while I'm here has me paranoid it's no surprise at all, that I'd better fess up before he tells me he saw me somewhere.

"What," he asks.

"Yeah, a quick trip," I say.

"Wanna get together," he asks.

I'm exhausted from last night. I should be getting Salt and myself back to Phoenix.

"That'd be great," I say. The same-town-as-family guilt is strong in me.

"I'm at The Arroyo. You wanna shoot a round," he asks me.

"I think you're talking about golf."

"Yeah."

"No."

"Well, I've got to play. I'm rusty. You can ride along."

"In the golf cart, you mean?"

"Yeah, the burger's good," he says.

And I'm so accustomed to accommodating male narcissism in my family that I accept my brother's offer of watching him practice my least favorite game in order that he may better impress clients, while my best friend waits on me in a coffee shop.

"How are you," he asks me.

"You been talking to Dad," I ask him.

"Not much. I think I might stop talking to him, stop . . . everything."

"Really," I ask. This shocks me. I always thought of James' personality alignment with you, Father, as something more, a philosophical agreement. But perhaps it's been even harder for him to tolerate you, your shared proclivity for black and white thinking meaning that while I'm busy probing my motivations for my own culpability in our malfunction, fretting over my philosophical imperative to forgive, he has no qualms about cutting your ass out of his picture.

James whacks the shit out of a golf ball with one of two clubs I can name—driver. "Damn," he says, as it slows and curves, well short and right of the green. It's unbelievable to me that hitting a ball that hard doesn't get it nearer the goal.

"Being with him is toxic," he says. "I've got kids. I don't want that for them."

"Gotta save yourself. "

"Yeah, man," he says, whole-heartedly agreeing with my half-assed two-bit wisdom.

We're back in the golfcart now.

"Shandy," he asks, holding up a *Leinenkugel's Lemon Shandy*, as he pops one open for himself.

"God no," I say, laughing at him. I love him. I wish I could enjoy one of those. Even if I did like it, I couldn't muster the self-possession to admit it, couldn't enjoy enjoying it, so powerful is the mixture of the habit of self-conscious self-judgment taught by you, Father, plus the categories of my cool-kid milieu.

"You don't think I need to honor him," he asks. Ah, there's the shame. There's the legacy of spiritual abuse, linking sons to abusive fathers, allowing their toxicity to grow ever greater, as it links battered wives to their abusers. No, that isn't all true: we sons are men and therefore holders of some agency, always, within this patriarchal shit pile.

"I don't," I say.

"Would you say that to a congregant?"

V

"Oh. No. I, uh, don't have any of those anymore. I quit the church."

"What?" James is shaken. "When?"

"Not long ago. It's been a bit of a whirlwind. Sorry. No, I'm not sorry. I'm trying to stop apologizing for the things I need to do to survive. And I think I've needed a little silence, a little space, to get through this."

"Do you still . . . believe?" I can hear the fear in his voice. I imagine he's wondering about the implications of my spiritual cataclysm on his own beliefs, on your, our father's, beliefs. I was the first of us to *come to faith*—am I the first to leave?

"Not in that church."

We sit there in the golfcart, on the path alongside his ball, for some time, as I wait on what's next.

"Wow," he finally says. "What's Leah think?"

As I grunt, I look out at the impossible rolling green of the golf course in this desert. "Damn," I say. "Maybe that's why I hate golf."

"What."

"Remember when Dad took us out to the golf course to tell us he was divorcing Mom?"

"Yes," he says, such surprising sadness in it—in this moment, he sounds like a man so much older than himself, so much more crushed by life than the ever-positively thinking overachiever I know him to be—as he looks out to the green, the jagged mountains.

"Maybe that's why baseball in person is, has *always* been, worse to me than on TV," I say. "Fresh cut grass is a terrible smell to me."

"I wonder what he was thinking then. That it was all for the best, probably."

"That his authority and wisdom were inscrutable. Even if his current worldview calls divorce a grievous sin; and that worldview, also, is inscrutable."

James laughs complicitly.

"I didn't answer you about Leah. I need some time before I talk about her," I say.

"Wow, okay," he says. "Are you okay?"

"No. I'm here without her. On a road trip alone, trying to get myself together. I haven't been okay in a very long time. But I'm more okay not being okay," I say. "Maybe I believe that."

James reaches for some iron or wood. I stop him.

"I've been thinking about our childhood. I know you're sorry for beating me up all the time. I can sense that. And it means a lot to me. But. Getting tortured, all the damn time, for years, for nothing, really fucked me up." I have to keep my eyes on the mountains, away from him, away from the golf course grass, to get through this with little enough crying to be intelligible.

"Brother, I wish you hadn't hurt me so much," I say, and turn back toward him.

"I'm sorry," he says. And I am sorry to hurt him, as this is obviously doing.

"I never wanted to say it fucked me up but now I see it did. I'm not gonna move past it without saying it. Dad never stopped you. And that's not your fault. But man, having your heroes treat you like that. And you two were heroes to me, of course." I am surprised to see him smile sadly at this, that some part of him is glad to know I thought of him this way. I suppose he let himself down too.

"I'm starting to see it made me believe I deserve to be treated badly," I say. "I see I've played it out all over my life, always believing the righteousness of the shit I'm dealt. Never letting myself enjoy any good thing."

"I'm sorry," he says again. He is crying. I am as surprised by this as I am by the fact he's mounted no defense, no "man up" blame-shifting bullshit.

"Okay. Alright. Thank you, I guess."

"I was a really fucked up kid," he says, and I can see this realization has been hard won for him. He's been on his own journey away from your habits of thought and action, I realize, which I'm only now glancing.

"I know. Dad made you feel powerless and you needed to feel powerful somewhere. His was your only model for power: domination."

James nods for some time, honoring me by taking this in.

"Raising Gus has been so strange," he says. "It's been hard lately, ever since he turned three, really. I felt like Mom and Dad, and Wayne, were such great examples of how not to do parenting, I was sure I'd do it completely different, had been mentally training myself on it for years whenever I thought about having kids. I'd made up my mind to be in a *relationship* with my kid. But man, when Gus won't listen to me, I forget all that. I transform into Dad. All I care about is forcing him to do what I fucking say."

"You can't just undo all that conditioning."

James nods. I hug him and I walk off on a path pointing across the fairways and greens, bound to interrupt multiple meaningless games I hold in self-conscious contempt, aiming myself toward the pro shop.

"That doesn't feel like the end of this," he shouts.

"No," I yell back. "But I'm good for now."

"Are we okay," he asks.

"Yes, Brother," I call back.

VI

49

My Leah

FATHER, I'VE BEEN PUTTING off telling you about Leah and me, biding my time and stoking my anger against you, journaling what ugliness or beauty I think you'll see in me. I've written so as to avoid writing the deepest truth. Here I am, at the end of my overdeveloped capacity for self-reflection, my somewhat more limited capacity for polemic. And I want, at least I want to want, to give you the whole truth—that I may receive your most accurate rejection.

I wonder if Leah's parents have gotten desperate enough to call you and you've just been so dumbfounded by your disappointment in me as to maintain silence between us. They shared the kinship of conservative Christians dismayed by their socially progressive offspring with you, but the alliance was shaky, their Reformed corner of the faith a bit put off by the lovelessness in your evangelical hard-lining.

Reading this without the details of what happened in my marriage, I imagine you've thought the worst of me, which I haven't corrected, because I think the worst of me. I must now be honest about Leah.

I've said over and over that I left her. That is my lived reality, shame gut-deep from doing something I was sure I never could. But I know the phrase paints the wrong picture. I'll resist the temptation to apologize—it's my instinct to apologize for everything, with you most of all. What I've done is mislead you into feeling what I've felt: that I am irredeemable. Perhaps I knew I could only trick you into empathy, twisted empathy though it is.

Leah had been working long hours since I lost my paycheck, logging miles daily on the 10 to and from Santa Monica. On a Tuesday, she got in a wreck on her drive home. I'd long feared such a wreck, in the most desperate hours of our marriage briefly hoped for one, then hoped instead for my own death, before quickly, obsessively, praying to take back all the death hopes. I have more compassion for these dark fantasies now, on the other side of church life; if God decides the thing with the finality of death, you're off the hook for that worst evangelical sin: agency. I'd be off the hook not only for a great sin within my church tradition, but also our family's gravest generational sin, the one on my mind since the moment I converted, in the aftermath, and because of, your divorce of my mom: the breaking of marriage vows.

When I got the call from the hospital, I was sitting on a park bench looking at Echo Park Lake, thinking how grateful I was to Leah for putting up with my faith deconstruction, cleaving to me and losing friends and family in the process. Despite our difficulties, despite my habits of mind, I was busy with gratitude in the hour before that call. Visions of how to construct a special evening—I was thinking sushi, her favorite, which we could never afford—danced in my head. The gratitude thickened the pace of the day and my mind wandered.

We sublet a bedroom in a friend's apartment overlooking the lake for a year before we moved into the big Kensington House, just a few houses over. It was the only time in my many years in Echo Park I had a view of the lake and during the entirety of that year, the view was of a draining, drained, and dredged lake, as they were rehabbing the long-toxic ecosystem. In the emptying of the lake, they found a parking enforcement boot, a pay telephone, an 1880s wagon wheel and, somehow, only three guns. There was heated local disagreement on this point. To be clear: the draining initially revealed two guns; the subsequent dredging revealed a third. We would look out our bedroom window at the Caterpillars sitting on the dry lakebed, craning and blooping in reverse, and laugh. It was our first year of marriage, our *honeymoon,* and we were looking out to our *view,* the barren moonscape of Echo Park Lake.

But the dredging was worth it; the lake I was looking at when I got that call was recognizable as a lake. The resetting of the grasslands had the lotus beds thriving once again. I was sitting in the afternoonness, my eyes on the Lady of the Lake statue, set up across from the Angelus Temple, home of evangelist Aimee Semple McPherson. She planted those lotuses in the 1920s, sometime between preaching to fifteen thousand people a day, seven days a weak, healing hundreds, and going through bipolar swings that had her sleeping with Milton Berle and faking her own death.

Gratitude thickened the pace of the day. I looked at the Echo Park parents strolling their babies and was grateful for them, zero envy in it for once; the lake seemed less an incoherent chop, and more a force of sustained direction, undulating its light toward me, the fountain mist, falling from a hundred feet high in the middle of the lake, exposed to afternoon sun and rainbowing down in sheets.

The hospital call hollowed me out, as it thinned out the day, pulled me out of nature and down into my phone, eyes anxiously upon it, expecting push notification of what I don't know, even as I sped away to the hospital.

I arrived at the hospital before the first of many emergency surgeries for her, at a time when the doctors still spoke in hopeful terms. Since we Christians pride ourselves on out-hoping everyone and especially doctors, it wasn't much trouble for me to *stay positive*.

On that Wednesday, Leah suffered catastrophic bleeding in one of her surgeries. The next day I was told there was no chance of recovery. She had experienced "what we used to call brain death," one of her doctors told me. I don't know for a fact what he hoped to accomplish by invoking this apparently verboten term but I guessed it was the extinguishment of hope. Which I think he saw as a mercy. I imagine, like I have, he has seen hope at deathbeds coerce, seen us piss away the chance to mourn with the dying by just naming them as much, seen us lose the chance for preparation, for ritual. What do you do when you've believed with all you've got that all you need to do is pray harder, believe better, for your dying love, and yet she dies? You blame yourself, you blame God, you blame her. Or you hope for an impossible return. We believe in the literal resurrection of the dead, for God's sake. All these blames and hopes, it seems to me now, are foolishly misplaced.

"What we used to call brain death," he said.

Mercy the doctor was providing, I stepped into a fighting stance and balled up my fists. He didn't flinch or defend. He pursed his lips ruefully, and waited to get hit. I collapsed into his arms.

Leah's parents were there by that Thursday, praying with me, sitting with Leah. They were present for most of the conversations the doctors initiated about ending life support and, as you'd expect, wouldn't hear of it. In a hospital setting, the subtlety and intellectually can drain right out of our Reformed categories, drive us quickly down to the blacks and whites of our evangelical roots, where a heartbeat must be fiercely defended as a life, from all comers. This happened for Leah's parents as I'd seen it happen for many others in my care as a pastor.

"She is stronger than you know," her father said to the doctors, again and again.

He was right, of course. She was stronger than I was in everything we ever came up against. But.

After a week of whipping myself back into a faith that believed a purity of belief could be my petition to God, I was exhausted and my little evangelical rekindling was smothered anew. I knew I wanted to let Leah go, and that it was my right, but I didn't have nearly enough strength to mount a counter-argument to her parents' relentless and smothering hope. I just sat there in that room watching them cry over their daughter and the protection I didn't provide, that particular grief a point of communion between us, *protector* stubbornly still a category for my self-understanding.

No matter what I come to believe, it will never be that Christians are idiots, because Leah was a Christian. The way she peered at you when you were explaining yourself made you feel doomed to failure, not because it was a stare of judgment—she had far less of that than I did—but because those eyes contained worlds—of questions, of counter-argument, of love. Her jaw was almost always tightened in a ferocious curiosity to match her eyes, which cut like knives. Which I avoided like knives in arguments, knowing that if I let them tractor-beam lock onto me while I was attempting to construct a coherent thought, I'd instantly see my ideas as nonsense and shut up, in fear I was about to start speaking actual nonsense. Such was the power of her disarming.

Lying in her bed for that week, her jaw was slack, propped open by her swollen tongue, the breathing tube crust-bloody in her nose. I would hold her hand, also swollen from all they were putting in her. And of course it all felt just as it did with my mother, or like Juliana or both. The same tubes, same swelling, same blood, same hospital, same fate, same God. I sat with her, ten hours at a stretch, nodding asleep, dreaming her awakening, only to awaken myself, to the same image of her as in the dream, except still-swollen, except never responding, except gone, gone, gone. It was clear to me this was the new her—this was the penultimate stop on a train to the desert, the wasteland clearly visible from this last outpost, itself a mustering point for the depredations of the wilderness, the city eons behind—that this was no her at all, never again could be. To delay a departure from this station is not to reverse course. A slowing of rot ought not be mistaken for the miracle of resurrection.

On the other side of being a pastor, it's not surprising that we, who believe our God man was raised from the tomb two days on, would not just believe in the mysterious possibility of, but come to expect, feel entitled to, such miracles in our own lives. We forget that belief in the resurrection is insanity; even if believed, it must be believed within insanity, as a constant inconsonance with the world. We believe in it like we believe in oatmeal.

Before, with Julia and my mother, who were not healed, were not raised, there was a tedious interrogation of my faith—even as I counseled others not to fall prey to it—did I not believe enough? No, that can't be it; I'm not one of those Prosperity Gospel people. God has a plan, and so shouldn't things make sense? Yes, according to church; no, according to all of life as lived. Is God withholding? No, intellectually; YES, experientially.

Now, such entitlement and subsequent bereavement seems to me not only theologically foolish but also a natural outgrowth of Christian culture, which promises prosperity, if not of material things, at least of God's Favor. Also, it seems to me the opposite of faith.

Shortly after Leah's parents woke that seventh morning, her hand in mine twitched. I blinked and shook, confirming this was my waking reality. They celebrated. As soon as I could escape their congratulations, I fled the room, the wing, the hospital, the bar, the city.

It's a couple weeks I've been gone and I'll be returning soon, I know. I didn't drive to New York; even though I've gone away, there's only so far I could stretch my orbit from her. Perhaps my actions seem no better to you now, perhaps kissing another woman while your wife is brain dead is worse still than whatever particulars you'd filled in. I sympathize with this view. You can always count on me as a partner in kicking me around.

50

Less Home

I WAS GOING TO drive Salt back after I saw James but I end up leaving him at the Vegas airport and covering his ticket back to Phoenix to get his car.

"I need to go home alone, I think," I say. And he doesn't argue. He waves a hangdog goodbye at me after I've hugged him.

Home, I say, home it will always be, although I've lived now as many years away from Phoenix as I did in it, although my mother is dead and any house I ever lived in is not only long-abandoned but bulldozed, although you and my stepfather, the least familial family I could count, are my only relations left in town. Although the purest and most stable family experience I've had wasn't in Phoenix but LA, not with my family of birth, but with my chosen church family. Which I blew up myself.

"You heard of Richard Rohr," I ask Salt.

"Yeah," he says. Salt always read more spiritual literature than I did.

"I think I might go to a retreat of his," I say.

He nods affably, humoring what I think he thinks is foolishness. But maybe, I'm beginning to ponder, he doesn't judge me as harshly as I judge myself.

As I cross into Arizona, James calls me.

"Remember Dad and the Minotaur," he asks. "I was thinking about that today after you left. Of how I don't want to be as a father."

"Yes," I finally say. "I remembered Dad's explosion, I've thought about it often. I just couldn't remember what it was about. Thank you," I say, as he has provided a precious puzzle piece to this memory, even if the fuller picture makes even less sense.

The Minotaur was another one of your lines in the sand, Father. James was excited about Greek mythology in middle school; he was rarely excited about learning; I was the academic one. This was just after the divorce, making me ten or eleven. He was rambling, floridly, about all these curious gods and creatures. And for some reason, when he came to the Minotaur, you forbade him from speaking further. Something about the Minotaur, versus Artemis or even Hades, was particularly offensive to you.

James kept talking and when he began a more detailed physical description of the Minotaur, you slammed the brakes of that old Audi and pulled over on the side of Bell Road. Perhaps you were afraid of the Greeks and their sexual preoccupations, worried where things could head if an anatomical description included the genital. Most curious to me, this was years before your evangelical turn, when you still extolled the virtues of a wide-ranging liberal arts education. But even then, I suppose, the neither-fish-nor-fowl nature of this beast, his even splitting of two categories, his failure to be blackable or whitable, was deeply unsettling to you.

As cars flew by at fifty, you jumped out of the driver's side, ripped open James' door, leaned over him to press his seatbelt release button, ripped him out of the car by his shirt, and slammed the door so hard the ash tray flew off its brackets, across the car, hitting my door with a *ting*. I watched you scream in James' face, misting spit upon him, waving your arms histrionically, as in some Dadaist caricature of masculine rage, which seemed not masculine at all, made you look more like a clownish heel (the Bushwackers, of WWF of yore, come specifically to mind).

When you were done, James got back in the car and apologized in somber tones, his face in shocked disbelief. I accepted his apology in equally performative tones, attempting to play according to the rules reset, as they constantly were—new absolutes replacing old and mutually exclusive absolutes—by your ridiculous behavior. Which we didn't, couldn't, know was ridiculous. You were a god to us. We must have just been missing some key to render your behavior explicable.

I already knew what a Minotaur was, Dad. He was featured prominently in that dumb Jason and the Argonauts stop-motion movie we loved as kids and had been watching for two years on repeat.

∾

I am in Phoenix, drinking a beer and eating a burger. I'm vibrating with energy and anger, have been since I left James to return here. There are TVs tuned to both CNN and Fox News in the bar. There's a caravan coming, of Central Americans hoping to escape violence, of rapists with Middle Easterners sprinkled in, Trump says. A caravan! With possible jamboree to follow. And if that happens, well brother, a hoedown is virtually guaranteed.

This from the party that brought us the evil genius messaging of "death tax" and "tax relief." What have you done with your A-level linguists? They left the party along with all capable of critical thought?

51

Return

I PULL UP TO Wayne's house unannounced the next morning; one may forego phoning ahead when visiting a shut-in. I get the zipper-cased pistol from the trunk and sit with it in my lap, in the driver's seat, looking at his front door. I know those door handles, long and copper, patinated by weather and palms, stolen with pride from the front door of the Scottsdale Trader Vic's, Wayne's and my mother's favorite restaurant, when it closed down. Ripped too, apparently, from the giant front door of the home we shared together prior to demolition by its contractor-buyer.

I get out of my car and stand on the porch, a jangly mess: antique toy soldiers, a massive cross section of a petrified tree, multiple chess boards, the bench swing he never got around to rehanging. He gave me, and read to me, my first book of poetry, Frost, I think, on that bench swing. I also remember him sitting there with my best friend in fifth grade, Daniel, explaining the ways of the world to him as they waited on Daniel's dad to pick him up. It was the night of my twelfth birthday party, a sleepover that ended early because Wayne taught Daniel a lesson by whacking him in the forehead with the prized pool cue Daniel had been mishandling. Wayne did this to us regularly, a blazing fast and tightly controlled strike he could pull back at the last moment, giving you a gust of wind to the face, or pull back just past the last moment, giving you a light, but fiercely intimidating, crack with the edge of the apex of one knuckle. Or the felt of the tip of a pool cue. Wayne's expert control was no comfort to Daniel, who cried and cried. "You're not hurt," Wayne said. "What the fuck did you to my son," Daniel's father said, upon arriving. This I heard from inside the house, behind that front door.

Wayne has been reclused for the decade since his divorce from my mother, abandoned as lost, finally, by Alexander, my close ex-stepbrother, for seven or eight years now, taken care of since by my other ex-stepbrother, Rick, with whom I was never close. Wayne was always an alcoholic, periodically functioning.

These last fifteen years of his sixty-five he's been a fulltime drunk, any attitude of maintenance—of relationships, of work-life, of the joy in the relative highs of an elevated BAC or the relative lows cobbled out unto moments of clarity—gone, in favor of the acknowledgement that the drink is poison, poisoning is the goal, the arduousness of the task of achieving a toxic dose another mountain to climb, like banking his first million by thirty-five. For all his differences, Father, he is goal-oriented like you.

Fifteen years ago, due to what I don't know except that my mother blamed herself for it, his character-defining disappointment crested into despair, and his pursuit of death via alcohol began in earnest. I marveled continually at how he'd lived through it this long, this long, *this* long, now fifteen years long. I wonder if it was a marvel, or a bitter frustration, to him too. Catching his fulltime disease is what eventually triggered my mom's survival instinct and sent her running for divorce. Just a few weeks of being back in it with him, after he'd snuck back into her house, was enough to destroy her. And here he's survived his grim devotionals, yet another two years.

Rick answers the door. He is gaunt, and I worry about him, about whether these days the drugs are edging into the scary place of mostly hard or clinging to the sad hope of mostly soft, and about his anger, as I always did growing up.

"John," he says, astonished.

"Hey, Rick." I say. "I'd like to see your dad."

"I, uh, dunno if he's up to it," he says. "What you got," he asks, gesturing at the zipper case I am cradling in both hands, as one does an heirloom.

"Yeah. A gift."

Rick reads me, for malicious intent, I think, which he doesn't seem to find. How much violence is in us men; he isn't wrong to think the love and the hate between Wayne and me could all swing wildly off kilter if we aren't all careful here.

"Okay. Uh, wait. Okay, come on in," he says, and entering, I see one reason for his stutter.

The place is a mess of cats and cardboard boxes, Rick's beer cans and cigarettes, Wayne's discarded off-brand plastic vodka handles.

"Can I get you anything," Rick asks.

"No, thank you," I say.

Behind the stacked refuse are the mementos: gorgeous antiques worth thousands—it's my understanding they get by on social security and disability—from Wayne's profligate spending years. He and my mother shared the extravagance you and I have despised. Trophies for his martial arts and bodybuilding achievements, photos of the good old days in real estate and with my mother, also clutter the space.

Here they are, on their wedding day, shoulder padded and quaffed into giddy smiles, my mother, in her early forties, still childlike in her beauty to me. I am somewhere just out of frame, in the prime of my chubbiest year. I had, I have, her cheeks. God, they were beautiful, sunbaked people.

"He's not really up to it," Rick says.

"I'll wait," I say.

Rick smiles at that.

"Still stubborn," he says.

"Yeah, sometimes," and I am smiling warmly back at him. "How are you?"

He shrugs, his shoulders half-gesturing a *you're looking at it* to the space around him.

"I'm okay," he says, salvaging decorum. "Let me see."

I barely have the time to get lost in a painting of a wild stallion under a setting sun, lost in my memories of this painting, from the house we all shared together like everything hanging on these walls, before Rick nods me into Wayne's room.

"He doesn't look good," he warns.

And dear God is he right. Wayne is a far sight worse than he was two years ago at my mother's memorial dinner. He must be about 110 pounds, this man who was wrapped in muscle like a winter coat under his t-shirts, well into his forties. It's the first time I've seen him in a decade that I haven't felt even a momentary joy in knowing that I could beat him, that I am the stronger one, I am the *double tough* one now. It's been almost twenty-five years since those nights he had me cowering in my room while he menaced our home, our things, my mother. I know, I never admitted, but now I know, that I lifted all those weights, which I was taught to do by him, broke skin and noses and ribs against bags and boards and people, all so I could be powerful enough to beat him, a power that, once attained, went unspent, gave me nothing but bad dreams. It did get James off my ass, though; he stopped trying to hurt me once he doubted whether he could win.

Wayne is shaking as he leans up to look at me. It seems there is a neurological component to his alcoholic demise. He leans on the same brass post bed he had when he and my mom were first together—which went to my stepbrother in adolescence and back to him in his old age—in which we all watched bad movies on cable. It was here in this bed, at ten, that I saw my first breast, my pure excitement quickly muddled by the setting, a horror scene of casual cannibalism, grimmer still for the cheapness of the production. The breast was *fake*, Wayne told me, which could be ascertained, he informed me, by the rigidity of the breast in question. The secret knowledge of this sorting skill, I understood Wayne to say, was vital to my coming of age. C.H.U.D II, an experience, like so many Wayne memories, full up with wonder and horror. And now I am full up with contempt for him, undiluted by love, a rare feeling, thinking *goddamnit why*—why show me the things he did, trot them out on screens and in life, I was so innocent. Because I was innocent?

"Could you give me that?" he gestures at a pillow on the far side of the bed. I set the zipper case down on his bedside table and lift his head, feeling the massive absence of muscle even in his neck, where the tendons stretch, tense and lonely. I put the pillow under him, on top of two already there. He looks me up and down a moment. I am sad to see the pride in it. "Look in the radio there."

I open his bedside CD player/alarm clock/radio and inside is a CD Rick must have burned for him from my podcasted sermons at Redeemed, labeled "John, The Beatitudes, 1/4."

"I was listening to you just this morning," he says.

I've picked up the zipper case once again, am again holding it in my folded hands.

"I was proud of that series," I say.

He nods.

"First and last time they gave me four Sundays in a row," I say.

Wayne rattles and coughs. Touching his neck and his pride has derailed the momentum of my contempt.

"What's in the gun case," he finally asks me.

"The Colt," I say, the .45 automatic he gifted me. "Pistol and magazine, loaded and ejected. Cleaned it before I left town," just like he taught me the night of the first time he took me shooting.

He nods a little before grunting knowingly, cantankerously.

"It's your gun. I don't want it," he says.

"I have a question for you," I say.

"I don't want to talk about your mother," he says, as his voice gets shakier, the rasp in his throat flowering into a cough, which grows into a hacking cough.

"Not about her," I say, and hear, on *her,* my voice, too, has gone wobbly with emotion. I recover my footing by leaning away from the desperate sadness—thick in the molecules between us here, in the space of all these vacant years, in his body's dead weight.

"It's an old gun," I say, through gritted teeth, regaining a foothold in anger.

"They've made those Colts the same for a hundred years," he says.

"No," I say, and he turns toward me. "*This* gun. *This* is an old gun."

"Yes," he says, rolling his head away from me, toward the window.

"I need you to answer a question for me. I've been thinking about it for over a year now and we haven't talked in that long. So."

"Please go," he says. He is crying, I see, for which I feel nothing.

"I will."

"I need to rest," he says.

"You told me your dad killed himself when you were seventeen. How?"

Wayne slows down and breathes deep, controlled breaths.

"Did you gift me a suicide gun, Wayne?"

"You aren't superstitious. It was your favorite," he says.

"But you are, Wayne."

I shake my head at him. His strange breathing continues, as though he is mindfully undergoing a great ordeal. How unworthy, this father figure, you, Father, all men, have been in my life.

I'm glad we are here together, that he can witness the face of my disapproval blossom like a rose in time-lapse, rather than simply presume it, intellectually, in my absence.

"You knew me so well. You saw how depressed I got, and responded to me. You gave me the poems of Hart Crane and Sylvia Plath. They were such a comfort to me. Until in college I found out they killed themselves, was convinced you'd ordained that discovery. That hurt very much, Wayne. Thinking any gift you ever gave would become a sinister one, eventually."

He doesn't answer. I count five breaths as I wait.

"You understood me," I say.

"Yes."

"You must have known, a kid like me, a man like me, that I thought about killing myself. And still you gave me a gun, a suicide gun."

"I didn't know. Not for sure. I loved you."

He won't look me in the eye, casting his wandering gaze, his wondering gaze, all over the room. I put my hand to his cheek, turn his face toward me and put my eyes an inch in front of his, which don't stop desperately darting.

"You knew," I say, and put the gun case down next to him on the bed, before walking out, saying, "and that ain't love, Wayne," as I exit his bedroom. I holler a goodbye to Rick on my way out the house.

I start the Volvo fast and gun the gas, working to believe it's the power of my conviction propelling me. But I fill my cabin with enough engine noise, fill the space between Wayne and me with enough quick distance, to outpace or drown out anything that could call back to me from his bedroom, even a gunshot.

~

I drive to your house from Wayne's, the idea being to leave this volume on your doorstep, or ring your bell and punch you in the nose, I don't know. But I cruise right on by your place. I want to be done with you, want to capitalize on the father-figure disowning momentum I have going for me. It gnaws at me not to be done with you, to continue on in silence between us as I fill page after page with elucidations of our rupture, while leaving the work of rupturing undone. I often feel like a coward for not getting it over with. It's excruciating to live in the gray of feeling and writing these feelings, having not shared them. But I make the better choice, and point my car away from you, away from Richard Rohr, another old white man, back toward LA and my wife.

VII.

52

At the Lake

I DRIVE FROM PHOENIX to Echo Park without making a stop. I walk Leah's and my old neighborhood—our first apartment together, our old bars and coffee shops, the house I still live in, on paper at least, the lake. I allow myself to remember. Allow myself to mourn.

I welcome in the memories, all of them and all at once, this vibrant neighborhood that had grown dim in my spiritual and marital malaise, now vibrant again as I'm reconnected to what I'm grateful for in Leah, in my church family here, estranged as it may be. I pace the walking track around the lake. What a beautiful place the park is in the evening, all sunset gold and pink, yoga class and cart-vendor and children running and parents strolling and young couples holding hands.

The truth that I've been gone just a couple weeks is staggering. It is the same season and time of day as when Leah and I first moved here and walked the park together, samosas in hand, full of hope for our life together. And I feel hope here too, despite the fact it's death that's brought me back to Los Angeles.

"Hey, John," a voice calls, drawing my attention away from the tall grass bending in the shallow water. The voice belongs to Matt, a friend a subchurch member brought to group once. He never returned but he continued to meet me for coffee sporadically, which I always enjoyed. He is divorced. I assumed that's what kept him from belonging in our group.

"How are you," he asks.

I sputter a non-answer.

"Lost in thought," he says.

VII.

"I'm thinking about what depth I can speak at with you. What I can expect you to hear." He blinks. I nod. "How are you," I ask.

"I start shooting my first feature in a month!" Matt was a frustrated filmmaker, his angst ever hanging on his sleeve.

"That's great. I'm happy for you." And I am. "I'm back in town from Phoenix." There is a large purple RV, which a few people live in, parked next to the lake for something like two years now, which I see as I look away from Matt. "Purple Lives Matter" is painted on its side. The glibness of this joke has never failed to tense me up.

"My wife is dying in the hospital," I say.

"Oh, God," Matt says, covering his mouth.

"I need to go to the hospital."

Matt is nodding at me.

"Is it . . . Can I give you a ride? Or something?"

"No thank you," I say. "I'm gonna go now though. I am happy for you."

"I'll pray for you," he says. I don't have the heart to tell him how hollow and relationshipless those words seem to me now, have always seemed to me, really. I don't have the energy to wallop him with my faith deconstruction and try to fumble through handling whatever fallout it stirs in him. But I have no reason to think he didn't mean it as a genuine expression of care. He is a kind person.

So I smile and nod goodbye.

53

Hospital Beds

When I arrive at Leah's hospital room, her parents are gone. "Thank you, God," I say out loud, as earnestly as I have ever prayed anything.

The nurse is in her room as I enter.

"I'm her husband," I say.

"I remember," she says.

"I'm sorry. Renee," I read off her dangling badge.

"What do you need," she asks me, taking my hand. A sob begins in the hand she's holding, snaking up into my heaving chest and my head, shaking it paroxysmally as I weep and tremble all over. She has seen spouses in my position before, is well aware I might need what she can't give, and yet, has the reservoirs of compassion to offer it unreservedly. She probably knows what I need better than I do. I should just ask her.

"I need some time with Leah. I don't want her parents to come in," I say. "Is that . . ."

"I can arrange that. I'll call security."

"I don't know if that—"

"Just in case," she says sweetly, knowingly. Leah's parents antipathy toward me is well known on the unit, apparently. "We have counselors here. And legal advice. If you want to know more—" she wince/shrugs as she takes a moment here—"about your rights."

Because my throat closes at the thought of what plug-pulling disagreements she is anticipating, I shake my head *no no, God no.*

Renee nods sadly as she closes the door.

And I'm left alone with my Leah.

VII.

I stand facing away from Leah, at the closed door, putting my focus on my breath. Breathing and breathing and breathing. "I'm sorry," I manage.

"I shouldn't have left you. I mean I had to. And I know you'd have compassion for that, try to talk me into having compassion for myself. But still.

"I'm gonna turn around now," I say, within the greediest breath of my life. I breathe like relegating this task back to the autonomic nervous system would be life threatening, like there is no greater demand on my intellect and soul than to make sure this air gets moved in and out.

I breathe like the breaths themselves are the measure of some progress here, choo-choo train huffpuffs that will, in time, find me some station. As if there's any track left, any directionality, any destination.

When I've turned around, I am staring at my feet on the floor. I still haven't dared to see my Leah.

I laugh, for Leah's benefit, which makes me instantly self-conscious, as I remember I don't now believe there's a her here to collect that benefit.

"I don't know what I'm more scared of. That you'll be sitting there bolt upright, looking through me and into all my thoughts with your big eyes like razors. A miracle I've died for. Or that you'll be like I left you. Only three weeks further diminished." I don't have the guts to say out loud my third fear, that I will look up to see Mom, or Julia, that my grief, fear and doubt have finally clean broken reality.

"Here we go," I say and see her, just her, as I left her, undiminished and unresurrected. "I love you," I say, looking into her closed eyes, still razory, to my imagination at least. "I'd like to be more profound than that. But I was so hurt in our marriage, so scared. It is profound to me, to think and hear myself say even that much after all of it. How terrible that I needed to be here for it."

I pull a chair up next to the bed. I hold her hand. It embarrasses me, but I took a photo of my mother's and my hands together in her hospital bed, when it was certain she was dying and we were waiting on the courage to take her off life support. I was thinking one day, when the bitter sadness had dissipated and just mostly beauty remained, I'd have it painted for me by my friend.

"Holding your hand is nothing like holding hers," I tell my wife. "You look nothing like she did. Your wounds came from the outside in. Damn, honey, it's a lot of stiches." There are multiple treasure map arcs on her head, shoulder, neck. The one on her scalp is a horseshoe pattern, as though the doctor went off in the wrong direction and had to cut back.

I put my head on her shoulder and share her pillow. This is the first time I've smelled her scalp in a month. It is heavier and sweatier and more Leah than it's ever been.

"I came to you with so much pain. I needed you to be more than I had a right to expect. And that's because of where I come from, my mother and my father. And my stepfather. All pulling my heart—and mind and faith—in so many directions. Of course I was too much for you. You couldn't meet my demands because of *your* mother and *your* father. I've got new compassion for both us lost little kids. I'm sorry to both of them for not getting what they needed from the parents and spouses that should've loved them best. But Jesus, you tried for me. Like no one else. I know I didn't always credit your trying, got caught in the zero-sum understanding of compassion, operating like if I acknowledged your efforts, mine would lose out in the debate."

I get off her pillow, sitting some inches apart. I return to my breathing, looking around the room, marking her machines, the view out her window, the hills above Chavez Ravine, which are the next, bigger hills beyond the hills of our Angelino Heights. I want to believe I am remembering the space I'm in as a way of inhabiting these moments, not disengaging from them. But perhaps I do need some small break from staring my shattered wife in the face. It isn't long before I pull myself back to her, putting my head against her ribs, which smell less like her, more like these hospital fibers, hospital cleaners, hospital soap.

"I'm sorry I took away the stability of our church life at the same time I took away the stability of my paycheck. Meager as it was to my ambitions, we counted on it, and I was dismissive about the impact of losing it. Money isn't crass, as I know I made it out to be. I'm sorry I went from praying nightly with you to praying with you not at all. I did these things to a woman who'd grown up craving stability, a paycheck worth a damn from a church worker, which your father never could get. I was so focused on my need to get out of the church. I didn't think about how earth-shaking it must've been for you.

"But I have compassion for my myopia too. With pain that deep, of course I couldn't feel anyone else's pain, right then. But I'm sorry. No surprise there. You know me, always sorry. I do think there's less shame in my sorries now."

I straighten up in my chair, looking toward the door, now aware of people, husbands and wives beyond Leah and me, in this building.

VII.

"I know you'd be happy about that," I say, returning to her. "'You'd be.' Damn conditional tense, dipping its toe into the past tense. Do all the husbands on this unit use it? Jesus I wish I knew you could hear me." I breathe, my tears and breath achieving some flow with one another, the resistance ebbing. "Your health state and my faith state have me flunked out of hope. But it is good to be here with you. With your heart beating.

"That sleep psychologist told me they're learning the heart is a second little brain, that the neuron clusters there are similarly dense, and communicate with those in the brain, and that's why we can use our breath to slow our heart and calm our mind."

I put my hand on her chest and feel her heartbeat on my palm. My stream of tears has had me whispering through my words but her heartbeat, and the reminder that the last heartbeat I felt with my hand was Janey's, breaks me all the way down; sputtering, I lose the rhythm. I put my ear to Leah's chest, an intimacy a few degrees beyond what I could allow myself with Janey, a communion I owe to, want with, Leah.

"I've been lost. Running. Away from home like a child. I kissed another woman. I repent of it. No. No, I just apologize for it. To you, or the you that was, I don't know. In what sense are you my wife now. Every sense. That matters to me, at least. So yes, I apologize to you. You'd like her—Janey—is the funny thing. Whewwwww. Shit."

I nod and breathe. Nod and breathe. And breathe and breathe. I feel lighter on my shoulders and in my chest.

"God, confession is deeply conditioned. Even if the categories for it are deconstructed, if your absolution, even your consciousness, are impossible, I still got to do it. Or is the instinct toward confession inherent, and not just in us church people?

"I'm sorry about our last days. Those days I was leaving the faith and you were pulling your hair out. You needed to know if I still believed in the virgin birth, the resurrection, if I could still pray. I know my taking prayer away from you was a deep hurt and I'm sorry I needed that break from prayer before—just before—I lost you. I said I wasn't sure if anyone was listening to my prayers, and so prayer had become too painful. I just stammered at you when it came to the miracles. I didn't know, and the black and white evangelical categories of belief and unbelief had me thinking that if I didn't know that Christ's heart stopped beating for two days, then got jump-started to beat again, I couldn't, by definition, be a believer.

"But those are their definitions—your father's, my father's, all the fatherses—a *they* I won't let set the terms anymore. Christ remains what makes sense of the world to me. I laugh that I thought I ever could or ever would get rid of Him. When I'm not sure He's there, I still pray. Now. I'm sorry you missed that, by just weeks. But. My experience of faith is a stronger one now than it has been in years. I'm not saying this to make you happy. I admit that is, will always be, a basic drive for me.

"I pity those dudes if they need to believe otherwise, if they believe judgment of my faith is an intrinsic part of theirs. I don't think I hate them anymore.

"Maybe excising the patriarchy is a possibility for me, a long and hard operation, I know. But Christ is in me, irrevocably, at this point. Maybe those patriarchs have been the conflict and the doubt in me, butting up against my faith, never a part of it, never making it more secure, as I'd hoped, as they'd promised. Maybe being stuck in their categories, needing to reconcile their shame with Christ's love, was all that ever made me think I was doubting my faith. Maybe I never was."

I nod a long while at this thought, comforted.

"Well, regardless, it's been too many years. The whole place has been custom fitted around Him. I'm a white dude from Arizona who's spent his life looking through the lens of Christ. I'm not gonna start calling myself a Buddhist just because I meditate. Christ isn't something I even want to get rid of anymore. I like myself." That sets me off crying more sputteringly. "For someone soaked in shame so long, liking yourself is a revelation, even a hurt. Damn life is weird."

In looking for a break, this time my eyes lock onto the bank of LCD screens connected to her five IVs, the displayed chemical names and hourly dosages blue blinking at me.

"I have an answer for you now. I believe in the resurrection."

I breathe. "That is good to say." I breathe for minutes, for days like the seven days of creation if you are anything but the coldest literalist, days that are eons.

"John," Leah's parents both shout outside the room. Renee is good to her word, as I hear security, and her, fight them off. Her parents' yells are desperate and angry: what malevolence they've dreamed I'm up to in here. Evil lurking, always lurking, around every corner in their imaginations. Never goodness, never love, that jumps out to affirm their beliefs.

VII.

"I am with my wife," I shout so loud it shakes Leah and me, so loud her parents may have heard it far down the hall, as Renee has them by now.

"Leah," I say, to turn myself back to her. "I love your name. What your parents were possibly doing, naming you after the Bible's second-prize sister, aside. Whew. The resurrection, we were talking about. As dark as American Christianity is, has been, it's a blip. Billions Christ changed, billions, after He was crucified. In his life He reached a few thousand. Anthropologically, biologically, did His heart beat again, I don't know. Historically, Christ rose again, restarting time at year zero. He made charity a rule and not insanity. Which makes the heartbeat the lesser miracle. And so I don't have a problem believing in the heartbeat after all. Heartbeat," I say, and break down again, my hand desperately reaching out to her chest, and down to her breast, the sexually adjacent no longer walled off from the rest of life, the rest of me, it seems.

"I love your body. I'm sorry about all the shame you went through. I was so angry for so long with your treatment of me, some member of the patriarchy by virtue of my genitals and not my behavior toward you, I was so sure. So angry. That I was left carrying the luggage of the men who shamed you early in life. Who abused you. Yes, abused. Neither of us ever used that word together. I imagine you were taught, just like I was, to never *play the victim*. They abused you. And I'm sorry. I was also a victim of theirs, I've come to realize. I'm not at the nomenclature of *survivor* yet.

"Maybe I was playing the zero-sum game there too, unable to credit your hurts lest mine be silenced even longer than the forever I was struggling against. But I wasn't quite as easy a mark as you, always eligible, theoretically, to code switch into their in-crowd of masculine agreement. And even if I don't want to carry your luggage, my maleness does implicate me. My desire for you wasn't always pure, was sometimes violent, in its intent or conception, if not its physicality. So it isn't just a sorry of disembodied regret over your experience, after all, it's a personal apology. I played patriarch over you too, and I repent."

In this moment, there is something in the prayer that is my thoughts that brings me to a terrible holy insight. My mouth drops open before my speech rings out:

"I've thought *fuck all abusers*. But I see your pain more clearly now than I could let myself when we were together, when I was trying to win. Pushing my pain on you, for years, was an abuse. Fuck me—I say in prayer.

"Have you ever heard of self-compassion, John," I say, for Leah, for Janey, for some version of myself that loves even this darkest me.

I look in Leah's eyes, miracle believer I still am, will always be, waiting on something grand.

Breath.

Breath.

Breath.

Which does not come.

In the absence of that grandness I want to cut out of this gray and into the black and white, want to call Renee in to immediately begin whatever the plug pulling procedures are. But I keep my cut-offs at bay. I lean over her and kiss her goodbye for today.

54

"Just the alcohol,"

my stepbrother, Alexander says, kindly tending to the concern in my voice, when I ask "How."

Wayne is dead.

"He wanted you to do the funeral," Alexander says.

"Shit," I say.

"I know," he says.

"I love you, Brother," I say, laughing. "How are you? How's the family?"

"Great. I haven't had a drink or a cigarette since your mom died."

"That's great, Brother."

"Look, if you need some time to think—"

"No. I won't do it."

"I respect that," Alexander says.

"I love you, Brother. I'm sorry for your loss."

"Same here, John. I know you two had a special relationship."

"Yeah," I admit with a sigh. "Let's talk soon."

55

Living Room, Living Room, Living Room

It's all surface streets from Leah's hospital back to Echo Park. This is true of so much of my beautifully unexpected experience with artists in LA—freewaylessness on the east side. It's evening when I drive back, through the few remaining ungentrified blocks south of the 101, along-side the lake, past the old Anglican church and its big church bell, which remains still as loud speakers play a tape of a church bell ringing, onto Kensington Road and Angelino Heights. *Angelino Heights,* a name that un-derstands those rolling hills as the peak place we could hope to live—it did feel that way to us, some strange arrival we snuck into by virtue of luck and rent control—a name that framed us as angels.

To my home. It is my home. I will call it home, even if I've been unable to bear the pain of claiming this now lonely ghosted place as my place.

Parking the Volvo outside the Kensington House is an ordeal of crowd-ed memories. I haven't been here once since I left Leah and I'm afraid to return to it alone. I see myself, inside, worrying over every inch of it, like a hundred year old crumpled man, which is the spirit animal inside this thirty-six year old frame, I've decided, picking up knickknacks and outright trash and weeping over them, shuffling a Parkinsonian shuffle born of a purely emotional tremor, around this place we shared so much good and bad. This is also where the good and the bad of my extinct church community live; I'll open myself up to being haunted by that death too, when I enter.

But Salt is there in the kitchen when I walk in, drinking coffee at the table where we've shared so much coffee, and prayer and laughter and pain.

VII.

He is the opposite of a ghost in my life, a friend whose friendship has only grown stronger and truer after I did all I imagined would push it from me.

"Hey," I say, bewildered, snowblind.

There's people over, I can hear. They are praying in the living room, the sounds of group prayer in that room's tone unmistakable to me. Salt sees my face, which judging by his reaction to it, is terror struck.

"We had a meeting planned," he says, in the low wavering tones of apology.

"We."

"I've been meeting with the community again," he shrugs sheepishly.

"The subchurch."

"A lot of the same people, yeah, but we haven't been naming it," he says. I can tell this means he's been leading the community. He is accredited by no seminary or denomination as a pastor, which seems obviously right.

My shock and worry and fear melt off of me as I nod. At least part of what I'm nodding is how impressed I am with my friend's friendship, his care for me apparent in his care for this community I was responsible for.

Salt peaks out the kitchen doorway and down the hall toward the living room, I think to make sure no one else is coming toward us until and unless I'm ready.

"What do you need," he asks me, which this time doesn't break me down.

"I'd like to go to the living room," I say, and stand there, nodding my head in the horizontal, disbelief direction, at what I just heard myself say. Salt understands these mixed messages just fine.

"Okay," he says and walks my shuffling body down the hall. "Friends, John needs us," he tells the community. "How can we pray for you?" I am sure this gathering was understood to most as one for Leah, a miracle-seeking occasion like many prayer nights I have led or attended.

I look around that room and I see so many loving faces I'm sorry I hurt, or I'm afraid I hurt, or I know I hurt because they were angry enough, even as Presbyterians, to tell me to my face. All those faces are smiling kindly at me now. I see no judgment on them.

"Would you please pray silently, friends," I ask.

In their agreement I sense some remnant of their spiritual deference to me, that I am still worthy of leading this one spiritual practice.

The requested silence is self-protective. I know these brothers and sisters would try not to offend. I don't think they would faith-shame me now.

But I can't take God and me, and Leah's physical and spiritual state, being shoved into the containers of language right now.

The two hours they pray and touch and cry quietly over me feels like ten minutes, feels closer and more connected than anything I've ever felt in communal prayer, even before hurting them and chucking my religion, feels like home.

56

Book Report

I AM ALMOST DONE reading this book on Salt's coffee table, in two sittings, a memoir by Tara Westover, the daughter of a religiously afflicted and deeply mentally ill father—Educated. The mixture of Mom's bipolar, Wayne's bipolar, your obsessive compulsive personality disorder (look it up), your emotional and spiritual abuse, Wayne's physical abuse of my mom, James' systematic torture of me, mom's alcoholic neglect, your religious mania, my religious mania, my desperate and unmet need for your approval, all have the mundane insanity in this book seeming so deeply and oddly familiar to me, a difference of many orders of magnitude in quantity, but not in quality.

I just read this bit, in the narrator's adulthood, after her escape from her outpost home and the abuse she suffered there, where she tells her mother the truth of her abuse at the hands of her brother, and finally, surprisingly, her mother believes her.

"I was your mother. I should have protected you," she says.

A flush of adrenaline shoots from the crown of my head to my toes, leaving every part of me singed by lightning as I weep, then punch the air furiously, hilariously, from my reclined position on the couch.

Apparently those are words I long to hear. Do I wish I could raise mom to apologize for Wayne, for you? Or do I want you, oh Confessionless One, to repent? Of the abdication of your duty to protect me from James, or from yourself? Or am I asking James, again, please, big brother, for once, stand up for me? So many offenders, no promise of any protector.

I suppose, as in childhood, that leaves the job to me. I suppose, as in childhood, I weep because I fear I'm not up to the task.

～

Ha! You can scratch that bit above, about Tara's mother coming to her senses, breaking the cycle of abuse in one beautiful eraser sweep, one Salvation Moment. Tara's mother and father end up taking the side of the abuser and banish her from the family, claiming demon possession, actually.

It provides a strange and real hope, to see this on paper, to shout at the page, *He's insane, Tara. Just leave. Stop going back for more abuse,* to hold in my hands the proof that other family patterns are as entrenched as ours, as hopeless. To believe God is reading my story, thinking, *John, just leave.*

57

Good Enough, Father.

As MUCH AS I long to bury our relationship—smother it and put it in the dirt, attend to it with whatever ritual necessary to bind it from haunting me—I won't be hand-delivering this letter to you, just as I won't be providing Wayne the ceremony my mother was deprived. I want to believe that's not eye-for-an-eye bullshit on my part with Wayne, but a rebalancing my better angels feel enlisted to serve, an acknowledgement that even though he does hold a claim on me, by rights he shouldn't. But if I'm wrong about my motivations, if it is just a fuck-you to him, I can live with that. I can stop soul-searching for my fault in the pain of the congenitally aggrieved men of your generation.

I will mail this to you and you can take it or leave it, dear Black and White One. Yes, I acknowledge the lack of shades of gray here. I want to believe I'm developing a capacity for compassion for all hurts, even yours, even yours of me. But for now, in this, I must employ your own categories with you. Take me or leave me, all of me, Father. Finally accept or fully reject me that I may live.

I've provided you no cogent defense, no treatise of personal theology. But I'm satisfied I'm here on these pages in higher and purer dose than I've been able to give you yet. Having an actual me down on paper and in your hands is good enough. I believe. I believe my Heavenly Father isn't threatened by me, by my doubt or by my sins. I am going to try to care less and less and less, gently and daily preaching it out of myself, what you think of me.

I said I wanted to divine what voice in my head is yours (versus mine, versus God's). It turns out this is too great a task for my finite consciousness, for, I think, any human mind. I believe God will forgive me my finitude.

I'm sorry I don't have conclusions for you or for me. I, too, find comfort in clarity. But the seeping of the gray tones into all my world was not so kind as to keep hands off the theological this time. At the end, I don't know if God is a personal force like the person I talk to every hour in prayer, or an idea planted in my mind, whether, if He is that idea, He's the one who did the planting. But because whatever He is, He isn't threatened by me, I am endeavoring to be unthreatened by myself, by my doubt, by my belief.

I'll be mailing this to you because I'll be here, my home, Los Angeles, preparing a funeral ceremony for my wife, seeking the help of a community I know I've hurt, with whom I have serious disagreements, but which I know loves us still, and will be a help to us. I'll be here paying a penance to my mother, the hero of my story, the rightful and robbed protagonist of these pages. I'll be here writing a sermon that is no slow-played altar call, is just my most faithful picture of my Leah.

What power I've given you, to let you dominate these pages and my thinking. I want to judge and punish myself for this grievous sin but even that instinct is driven by your categories. Instead, I'm going to borrow my mother's feminine compassion, for myself and for my wife, and believe I am good.

Perhaps that feminine compassion can stretch beyond the personal, launch into the cosmic and eventually return to the atmosphere of my beliefs, flaming upon reentry.

I will see.

I will meditate now on our Heavenly Mother, pray only to Her. Less as a corrective than as antivenom, medicine I need to live. Perhaps, some decades of prayer to Her from now, this will have God out of the containers you left me.

I see that Future Me, holding onto Her love with both hands, no longer groping for the shame, surreptitiously, with one loosed appendage.

I am aware that praying to God the Mother, like virtually all I do, is heresy to you. I am sad over that but not sorry.

I love you.

It's okay—it will someday be okay—that you can't see love as love. I still wish it for you, not pretending anger and even hate aren't yet intermingled with my love, but seeing the ratio tip in love's favor. One day, my mother

VII.

tells me, our Mother tells me, hate's last remnant will be burned up in love. After I've really let you go, probably. When the smell of fresh cut grass, and many other objectively pleasant things—no longer smells like shame.

www.ingramcontent.com/pod-product-compliance
Lightning Source LLC
Chambersburg PA
CBHW050403030726
47503CB00006B/2001